The

Girl of

Hawthorn

and Glass

The Metamorphosis Duology

The Girl of Hawthorn and Glass
Coming Summer 2021: The Boi of Feather and Steel

The Girl of Hawthorn and Glass

ADAN
JERREAT-POOLE

DUNDURN
TORONTO

Publisher: Scott Fraser | Acquiring editor: Rachel Spence | Editor: Whitney French
Cover design and illustration: Sophie Paas-Lang
Printer: Marquis Book Printing Inc.

Library and Archives Canada Cataloguing in Publication

Title: The girl of hawthorn and glass / Adan Jerreat-Poole.
Names: Jerreat-Poole, Adan, 1990- author.
Description: Series statement: Metamorphosis ; 1
Identifiers: Canadiana (print) 20200178822 | Canadiana (ebook) 20200178830 | ISBN 9781459746817 (softcover) | ISBN 9781459746824 (PDF) | ISBN 9781459746831 (EPUB)
Classification: LCC PS8619.E768 G57 2020 | DDC jC813/.6—dc23

We acknowledge the support of the Canada Council for the Arts and the Ontario Arts Council for our publishing program. We also acknowledge the financial support of the Government of Ontario, through the Ontario Book Publishing Tax Credit and Ontario Creates, and the Government of Canada.

Printed and bound in Canada.

VISIT US AT

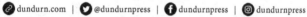

dundurn.com | @dundurnpress | dundurnpress | dundurnpress

Dundurn
3 Church Street, Suite 500
Toronto, Ontario, Canada
M5E 1M2

For Mom, who first gave me magic,
books, and feminism

One

Eli popped an extra-strength Advil and downed it with a mouthful of lukewarm coffee. She hoped that would stop the ache in her chest, although it would do nothing for the rattling cough that kept her awake at night. Bronchioles turning to thorns and spiderwebs were hell on a body. Eventually, she would turn back into the parts the witch had used to make her — a girl stitched together out of beetle shells and hawthorn berries and a witch's greed.

Eli took another sip of coffee and flicked her eyes to a corner of the café. The ghost had taken the form of a middle-aged man in Clark Kent glasses — he must have been watching old films to think those were still in style — and was fumbling with a MacBook. He hadn't touched his coffee, which was a dead giveaway. Caffeine short-circuited a ghost's nervous system.

She drew a dagger of glass, enchanted to be invisible to human eyes. Pasted on a nervous smile, the one she saw often on teenagers in the human world. Then she stood up.

It was time.

Eli wasn't just a teenage girl with heavy bangs falling over round glasses, fighting with her mother and writing bad poetry in her journal (although she did some of that, too). Eli was an assassin.

She bumped into Clark Kent's table as she walked past, spilling his coffee.

"Shit!" He grabbed his computer and jumped up, but not before some of the liquid had spilled onto his crisp tan pants. He hissed in pain.

"Oh my god, I'm so sorry!" Eli did her best squeal. "I'll get you some napkins!" She lightly pressed the flat of the blade against the back of his neck, reflecting the magic inward. Trapping the ghost inside.

Eli ran back to the counter to grab some napkins. "I'm sooo clumsy," she told the barista, who smiled sympathetically.

The blade had rendered the man docile. The body looked sick and confused. She'd never seen one so weak. Unless it was a trick.

Coffee dripped onto the floor — a lulling, rhythmic soundtrack to everyday murder.

Eli picked up the laptop, wiped down the table, and then carefully placed it down again. She eyed him warily, looking for evidence of the ghost. Sometimes they came out of the ears like steam and tried to escape, even when she used the glass knife. Hunting down a cloud of steam was a pain in the ass. This one seemed safely neutralized.

"You should go wash up," she told him. He nodded slowly. The man stood up, unsteadily, and walked to the bathroom at the back of the café. She followed him.

"I'm so sorry," she repeated, trying to remind herself to walk noisily, clumsily, like a human would. Her blades swung in a gentle, familiar rhythm at her hips.

Through the door, into a room with flickering fluorescent lights and dirty linoleum. The glaring afternoon sun pouring in through a window. A mirror reflecting their images back at them: a girl and a man. Hunter and prey.

Usually the ghosts resisted, and the trick was to keep them in the human body by magic and force. But this one seemed tired and ready to die. Eli wondered for a moment if she found that thought comforting — that she was helping him find peace. Exorcising the demon. Putting the body to rest. Then she shook her head.

She was made to kill.

She was created to derive pleasure in a job well done. And she was close to completing another assignment.

She pulled out a different knife, cloudy, its colour shifting and changing between greys, blacks, and pearl-toned whites. The man's eyes widened. "What —?"

Eli drove it into his skull. It went through easily, and she rooted around inside for a few moments, trying to catch the sleeping ghost. Trying to drag the magic out of its human shell.

Nothing.

Blood poured from the shattered skull, shimmering across her face like a red galaxy as she pressed deeper into his brain. The body collapsed on the floor in a heavy, meaty pile.

Eli stepped back, heart racing.

That wasn't supposed to happen.

Once she knifed a ghost, its body transformed back into what it was made from — a dog bone or an old biscuit.

This body remained stubbornly human. Eli heard footsteps outside the bathroom door and she was standing in blood, in the blood of the man she had just murdered — a *human* — and if someone saw her they would call the cops, they would track her down. Human bullets would hurt her as surely as they puncture holes in trees, and she would bleed, too. Even if she survived, her handlers would come for her and finish the job.

A thought jarred her out of panic: this man was the mark. She wasn't mistaken.

Which meant someone else had fucked up and put her here.

Fear and fury burned through Eli's body, making her cough violently as stone turned to ash in her lungs. (She had been warned about strong emotions.) Her hand tightened on the knife and she made the split-second decision to live. She was, after all, made to possess strong survival instincts.

As for the anger? That was entirely her own.

As the bathroom door opened, Eli threw herself at the window, cracking it with her elbow. She fell into the back alley behind the café. Taking a breath, she checked that her glamour was still in place — brown eyes, blonde hair, mouth heavy with lipstick — and that her blades were still shielded from human eyes. Then she forced herself to walk slowly into the bustling downtown, into the heart of the City of Ghosts.

Above the city, invisible to the human eye, darkening to a deep blue speckled with stars, hung the monstrous and magical City of Eyes.

Home.

Two

Once safely a few blocks away from the café, Eli ducked into an alley and let the glamour fall away from her body like dead leaves, tearing the last few pieces with trembling hands. It felt like a damp paper bag on her fingertips in the moment before it dissolved back into dust and dirt. Now she was herself again: poorly cut hair, pale skin with a few freckles, face flushed from the escape. The yellow eyes of a crocodile with black slits for pupils. Glasses that sharpened the world when her black eyes showed her the magic lurking in seemingly harmless things — a powerful tool that impaired her everyday vision.

Seven blades hung from a thick belt around her hips. All of them were killers, but the art of assassination required many shapes of death. There was the frost blade, the revealer, that cut through illusions and lies. The bone blade, the tracker, that took a piece of any body it touched and remembered its DNA. The blade of thorns, the ensnarer: when it pierced a body, the thorns would grow into a rosebush of pain and fury. The glass blade, the mirror, that harnessed the energy of an attacker and reflected it back on them. The stone blade, the shield — the largest and heaviest of the knives, almost like a short sword — that could kill as well as save. The pearl blade, shifting between white and black pearl: the divider, with the ability to separate the corporeal and the incorporeal, a knife that could tear magic from flesh, could hunt through any world or body or material.

And finally, the thinnest, sharpest weapon: the obsidian blade. Secret death. A blade that could cut through any magic. A blade that could destroy the most powerful beings in the worlds. The assassin.

Eli ran her thumb over the obsidian as she closed her eyes and prepared to cross the threshold between worlds. She blinked, and a new set of eyes replaced her reptilian pair. These were pure black, and through them Eli could see the border between worlds, could watch as a magical rift formed to carry her away from here. A column of shadow fell from above, and suddenly Eli couldn't see. It was pitch black inside the Vortex, but the quality of darkness wasn't like that of a darkened bedroom or claustrophobic closet.

It was the darkness of a sea that covered continents.

It was a darkness that whispered secrets from the past and future.

ADAN JERREAT-POOLE

Eli hung, weightless, the fragments of her glamour scattered on the pavement below in the human city, along with blood from the man now lying dead in a bathroom.

No human could cross the threshold.

The Vortex shifted, the core growing darker, as black as dead eyes and the hole in the head of a needle. The darkness threaded Eli through the fabric between the human city and the witch city. There was an uncomfortable tug, and Eli clutched her chest. It never got easier.

And then she was back, her feet on the ground, the afterimage of the alley fading on her eyelids, replaced with the painfully bright soil of the main square. Eli looked up at a different pattern of stars and, somewhere out there, the City of Ghosts. She had come so close to being discovered. To being trapped there. She shivered. The shiver wracked her magic-constructed body, but nothing broke or burned.

Eli sat down for a moment to catch her breath. The witch had not been entirely forthcoming about what had gone into the stitching of Eli's flesh, but Eli had figured out a few years ago that some of her components were human. It was why she was able to pass undetected among their kind. It also meant the Vortex fought over her every time she travelled between cities, welcoming only part — but not *all* — of her. She suspected some assassins were torn apart by the Vortex's magic or tossed back to the human city. She had never shared these thoughts with Circinae.

Witches and shadow-girls and great horned beasts moved through the streets without even glancing at

Eli. Her appearance was not out of the ordinary. A steel carriage pulled by jade steeds whipped around a corner and nearly ran Eli over, but she rolled out of the way just in time, wincing at the screech of stone on stone. She grabbed her glasses, which had fallen off, jammed them on her face, and forced herself to stand. Then, turning down the first invisible pathway her palms found, she prepared to weave her way through the back alleys and return home. Circinae would be waiting for a report.

The City of Eyes was overlaid with a maze that stretched across the city. The entrances, being invisible, were naturally difficult to find, but once she had learned to seek the scent of sea glass and dried blood, it was easy to slip away from the angry lights of the main square and the wide promenades that cut through the city like sheets of ice.

Checking that she had chosen the correct entrance-way and wasn't instead caught in a young witch's dream-world, Eli flicked out her lizard tongue to lick the wall. Seaweed and the corruption of dead fish. She sighed in relief and let her hand gently stroke its soft surface. In this part of the Labyrinth, the stone was the colour of snow tainted with a single drop of blood. Underneath her gentle touch, the wall shuddered as if in pleasure. Nothing in the witches' world was without feeling.

Eli's shoulders prickled, and she had that familiar feeling of being watched. It was a comfort, returning to a place where everything had eyes. Everyone was known, if only by a rotting branch or a luminescent scrap of architecture held up by faith and will.

"I missed you," Eli told the wall. A thousand invisible eyes blinked at her in welcome. Eli felt the brush of their eyelashes against her face. This was her home, more than the mossy structure where Circinae waited. Reluctantly, Eli removed her hand from the gentle pulse of the Labyrinth and started walking.

She had only gone a few turns before she heard her name vomited from the mouth of a taxidermy vulture, its body stolen from the human realm.

"*Eli lies, Eli dies, Eli sighs, Eli why,*" coughed and hacked the bird, perched on a branch of white iron that stuck out from the wall.

Eli crossed her arms and flicked her bangs out of her eyes. "Very clever, Clytemnestra," she said. "Did you miss me?"

A moment later, a little girl popped out of the wall, the surface stretching into a thin, slimy bubble. The bubble burst, and the girl shook her head, spraying Eli with water.

"Cute, isn't it? I stole that while you were gone. I tried to find you in the City of Ghosts, but you never let me see your glamours." She twisted her mouth into the shape of a pout.

Eli rolled her eyes. "If you stopped stealing from the human world, they'd let you join the Coven."

Clytemnestra grimaced. "The stupid old Coven. So many rules. Magic is meant to be chaos. Chaos is beautiful!" She threw her arms up in the air and the vulture exploded, splattering the walls with feather and bone.

"Now you've gone and ruined your plaything."

"I have other playthings." Clytemnestra smiled. "Won't you play with me, Eli?"

Eli shifted her body very slightly, preparing for a fight. "I'd rather not."

For a long moment the two stared at each other — the teenager with crocodile eyes and a human body, the tiny witch with a Cupid's bow mouth and sharp, sharp teeth.

Then Clytemnestra laughed. "Oh Eli, I missed you. Promise you'll visit again soon?"

"I always make the time to visit you, little one."

"Yes, well, I waited for *years* this time. It was boring." She frowned.

Eli didn't bother to correct her sense of time. She bowed slightly, not breaking eye contact. "My apologies, child."

"I forgive you! Oh, do come visit again. We'll have a tea party. Oh, and don't take the next right turn — there's an angry dragon-bird. Someone woke him up from his nap."

An object flew through the air. Eli snatched it and leaped back as Clytemnestra was sucked back into the wall. Eli felt the wall tugging on her clothing, but she braced her legs, and it sealed shut.

She looked down at what she held in her hand: a shard of bone china painted with blue petals. After a moment, Eli tucked it into her pocket. She had learned never to turn down a gift, especially from someone who might kill you one day.

Heeding Clytemnestra's advice, she turned left at the next fork instead of right.

Behind her, the remains of the vulture had vanished.

Three

Circinae had not always been called Circinae. Like all witches, she was born nameless and had to travel to the human world to steal a name.

"Mother?" Eli knocked exactly four times on the great charcoal door. Even the cottage door glowed with a terrible light, although not as harshly as the main square or the Coven. After a moment, the door crumbled into a pile of ash, and Eli carefully stepped over it and into the house. Behind her, the ash re-formed into a thick charcoal slab.

"Kite was asking for you," said Circinae, knitting something slimy into a scarf. She sighed. "Did you bring more?"

"When? Where is she?" Eli pulled out a handful of sugar cubes and placed them beside her mother.

"Good girl. How should I know? I don't ask such rude questions. Mind your manners — you're getting more human every day."

"I thought that was a good thing."

"Well, leave it in the City of Ghosts. You're keeping company with gods now. A true assassin can body switch *and* mind switch. You've always been stubborn. Too much granite."

"Yes, Mother."

"I expect we're to be summoned to the Coven shortly, so I recommend you wipe the smell of human off you."

"Yes, Mother."

Knit, purl, knit, purl.

"Is that all, Mother?"

"No. Where are my cinnamon sticks?"

Eli took them from her pouch and set them next to the sugar cubes. Circinae set down her knitting, picked one up delicately with manicured nails, and bit into it, crunching it like a bone.

"Don't you want to know how the mission went?" Eli asked quietly.

"You're here, aren't you? I assume it was a success. I didn't raise you to be stupid enough to come home a failure."

Eli hesitated. "Of course, Mother."

Eli stood there a little longer, the fire crackling purple, the shadows on the walls dancing like giant puppets. Her heart pounded against her rib cage, making a few buds bloom in her chest cavity. She clenched her hands. Took a breath in. Watched her mother for a glimmer of betrayal — sometimes, if you looked carefully, you could see the true colour of intention in the movements of the people who were supposed to love you.

Eli saw nothing. She exhaled. The summons had not yet come.

Not in immediate danger of being dismembered, she went to her room.

Once safely inside, she took Clytemnestra's gift and raised it to her mouth. Gently, she bit down, piercing a hole through the centre. Then she grabbed a piece of spiderweb from the ceiling and threaded it through the hole. She hung the fragment of china around her neck, the pendant hidden under her shirt.

A series of marks on the wall caught her attention. A perfect red circle to symbolize hawthorn berry. A few faint lines for spiderweb. A jagged line to suggest broken glass. Several other marks that meant nothing to anyone but Eli.

The recipe for herself.

Once she had thought to learn the secrets of her making. She had believed that if she knew the ingredients that made up her body, she wouldn't need Circinae to make her strong again.

Once she had even thought that this knowledge would free her. She had been reckless, playing a foolish, dangerous game. But she had given that up. She had accepted her place in the order of things.

She stared at the parts that had gone into her making and shuddered. This is what she would become if she were to be unmade. A collection of found things. Pieces of stone and glass. Circinae had raised her on stories of failed and disobedient assassins who were turned back into parts and repurposed. Or worse — fed to the Heart of the Coven.

And now Eli had killed a human.

Blood smeared across the tile floor. The look of terror in his eyes before the knife —

Don't think about it. Don't think about it. Don't think about it.

Heart thrumming, she turned away from the scribbles of a young girl. Kite had left an altar of moss and frostberries on the windowsill. Eli grinned, felt a warming in her chest, a dangerous furnace for a wooden house. She knew she should lie down on her own bed of moss and sleep. But Kite was waiting, and Eli knew where to find her. So instead she opened the window and slipped outside, feeling a different kind of thrill from the one hunting gave her.

These were the moments she lived for, morsels of stolen freedom.

Four

Eli had met Kite the first time she ran away from Circinae, back when she'd meant it when she called her "mother." Before she had learned that it wasn't a term of endearment: it was a title. (Eli reminded herself of that every day. She understood that creators have strings embedded in our hearts.)

She had run into the invisible maze, looking for shelter, imagining a secret hideout of other made-things, hungry and fierce and loving, who might rescue her from the witches.

She'd become lost in the Labyrinth. She was young, and young things are reckless.

"Come and play with me, little human!" A giggle from behind her. Eli spun around, but the wall was smooth.

"Over here, little girl!"

"This way!"

"No, the other way!"

Laughter dogged her steps, always coming from behind her. Eli could feel the eyes of the wall watching her, and she feared they were Circinae's. She didn't yet know that there were much, much worse creatures in the world than mothers.

Panicking, Eli closed her eyes. She felt the darkness of her lids like a gust of cool air. Now that her eyes were closed, she could not be deceived by the smooth, impenetrable walls, nor the curving pathways and elegant staircases that seemed to appear out of thin air to carry her in dizzying circles.

Eli pressed herself against the wall. She could feel rough patches and cracks. She followed one of the cracks, her fingernails digging into the porous surface, where moments ago it had been harder than glass.

By touch, she followed the crack for several minutes, until she realized the voice had stopped following her. As she turned a corner, she could feel that the crack was growing wider, and she could fit the tips of her fingers in it.

Soon, she could jam her hands in up to her knuckles. She felt earth and wetness. She knew, somehow, that this was leading her somewhere. Leading her out of the Labyrinth.

When the crack widened to allow her entire hand in, Eli stopped.

She felt eyes on her body again, and this time, they felt like a warning.

She's coming, they told her.

Eli started digging frantically, ripping out pieces of the wall, pushing herself into the dark, narrow crevice.

Closer.

She will catch you.

This is her world.

No. This is our world. Her world is outside our walls.

Stop, child, you're hurting us!

This isn't your home!

"This *is* my home!" Eli cried out, slamming her body into the wall. "This is my home!" She could hear the click of high heels on stone and took a run at the wall. She threw her body at the small hole she had made. "I *am* home!"

She passed through easily.

Behind her, the wall sealed shut, as if it had never been disturbed by the claws of a young assassin. Eli spat out a clump of dirt. It landed beside a pair of ballerina slippers.

Eli looked up to see the most beautiful child.

"Welcome home!" The child giggled. She offered a hand. "I've been waiting for you for ages. I eventually got tired and gave up, but here you are! Come, I'll show you the peepholes where we can watch the witches. This is going to be so much fun. I've never had a pet before."

Eli wiped her mouth and then took her hand. It was clammy and rubbery as seaweed. Lowering her head, Eli bit down hard.

The girl pulled her hand away. "Bad pet! Don't bite me!"

"You taste like salt," said Eli. "And I'm not a pet."

The girl hesitated and then knelt down beside Eli.

"You tasted me. Now I will taste you. This will seal our friendship pact."

Gracefully, she bent over Eli and bit her ear.

"You taste like life. And orange peels," she whispered. "Your name is Eli."

"How did you know that?"

"You told me in your blood. Can you tell mine? You have the taste."

Eli looked into the sea-green eyes for a long moment and then felt the sound bubbling to the surface, soft on her lips.

"Kite."

Kite exhaled. "Kite. *Yes.*" She squeezed Eli's hand. "You have entered the Children's Lair. Only children are welcome here. The walls and the Warlord keep us safe. You must not tell any adult about it."

"I swear it."

Kite smiled gaily and clapped her hands together. It sounded like a dying fish flopping uselessly on land. "Oh good. Now — let's play."

There was no day or night in the City of Eyes, just the pulsing dark of a sky that wavered between blackpurple and greygreen, the fierce glow of the city like a sun, and the twinkling lights of the human world somewhere overhead. Now the sky was acid green and black, sickly and spectacular. It felt like a portent, but Eli had never learned how to read signs.

Eli took the secret path to the island in the river. From there, she counted her steps — 115 north, 48 northwest — then spun around in a circle counter-clockwise four times. She plucked a hair from her head and offered it to the wind, who snatched it up immediately and devoured the dark strand. Finally, she closed her eyes and visualized Kite's stormy eyes and bird's nest hair. When she opened them again, Kite crouched before her, playing with a crustacean in a tide pool.

"What took you so long?" she asked. "I've been waiting *months*."

Eli didn't correct her.

"Got held up. Work, you know." She slid her hands into her pockets and leaned against a tree trunk, feeling, for the first time all day, calm. Kite had that effect on everyone.

(The calm that Kite carried with her was dangerous.)

"Here, I made you a snack." Kite blinked long feathery lashes that were like an insect's antennae and reached out, her palms flat and facing the sky. The crustacean was petrified, an icy bit of meat that Kite had coaxed up from under the riverbed.

"You know I'm always hungry after a mission." Eli grabbed the thing and threw it into her mouth, crunching a couple of times before she swallowed its sweet body. "Delicious."

Kite bowed her head in acknowledgement of the compliment. "Good hunting?"

"No." Eli sighed and picked at a stray thread on her jeans.

"The ghost escaped?" Kite's voice was like a lullaby, and suddenly all Eli wanted to do was lie down and sleep for years.

When Eli didn't respond, Kite moved forward, soundless, and placed a gentle hand on Eli's arm. Her skin was smooth and damp, like some kind of sea mammal.

"Eli?"

The touch and the voice made Eli's heart slow, her breathing steady, even as she fought the urge to pull Kite into her arms and burst into tears. But no — that would be the *human* thing to do.

"I don't know what went wrong," Eli whispered. "I'm worried I'm going to get unmade." Saying it out loud made it more real — and brought back the iron smell of human blood.

Kite's grip tightened, and a bolt of blue lightning sparked through her eyes. "I won't let that happen."

Two pairs of eyes: one animal, one storm-touched. Eli pressed her forehead against Kite's. "Circinae will kill me."

"It wouldn't be the first time," said Kite. "But we can stop her."

"What?" Eli pulled back.

Kite tried to look apologetic. Witches were notorious for not experiencing regret. "It was just something I came across in the Coven library. In the archives."

"Tell me."

"I can't."

"Why not?"

Kite drifted away from Eli and back to the tide pool. She began crooning softly, luring other creatures up from the depths.

"Come, let's have a feast."

Angrily, Eli walked over and stomped on the pool, sending critters scattering.

Kite sighed. "You have a human temper, Eli."

"And you sound more like Circinae every day."

Kite hugged herself and turned a hurt expression to Eli. "Take that back."

"Then tell me what you found."

"You know I can't. That information is only for witches."

"And I'm just a witch's pet. Is that what you're after, Kite? Trying to steal me from Circinae so you won't have to build your own?"

The thought had been creeping into her mind ever since that day, almost six months ago by human time, when Kite had left her on the island. That memory poisoned their time together now, and made Eli doubt every word Kite said.

"Maybe I'm just a toy to you, now that you're a full witch."

"That's not fair, Eli."

"And you're a shitty friend, Kite."

"I'm doing the best I can." Her voice sounded lost now, as if the sound waves were moving through water.

That was how Eli knew Kite was truly hurt, and in her fury, she took pleasure in Kite's pain.

"Well, I have more important things to do than feast and frolic today, Witch Lord," said Eli coolly. "So if that's all you can offer me, I'm leaving." She turned on her heel to walk away.

"I'm not the Witch Lord yet, Eli."

Eli paused and said quietly, "And when you are, I will lose you entirely."

Eli hadn't gotten farther than a dozen or so paces when Kite called her back, an inflection of fear in her voice. "Eli! Stop!"

Eli spun around, her hand already gripping her bone dagger. "What's wrong?"

Suddenly, Kite's magical body materialized in front of her, like mist come to life. She could move through the world like a fish cutting through the ocean. "A message. One of the animals brought it from under the riverbed." She extended an arm, her hand clutching a thick piece of bark.

"A summons from the Coven." Eli pushed her glasses up her nose and sighed. "They have the best timing."

"Be careful, Eli, the Coven —"

"Thank you for the summons, *messenger*," Eli said bitterly. "Now go back to your people and leave me alone."

This time, Eli didn't look back.

Five

Circinae was waiting, dressed in a long cloak of sewn-together leaves that were mottled brown and grey. "Why are you here? You should have gone straight to the Coven," she told Eli angrily. "They don't like to be kept waiting."

Last time Eli had gone straight to the Coven, and Circinae had been furious. Then she had punished Eli by refusing to show her the secret entrance to the Coven for several hours (only a witch could come and go as they pleased).

"My apologies, Mother." Eli took a calming breath and tried to push out the hurt and anger she felt after her reunion with Kite.

A thimbleful of guilt, acidic as bile, crept into her mouth. She spat it out. The glob of spit turned green and black, bubbled, and then was absorbed into the floor. The house thrived on powerful emotions.

"Let's go already." Circinae spat on Eli, her own saliva red as blood. It spattered across Eli's face and stung, but she had learned as a child not to flinch. Magic always hurt, in one way or another. A witch's skill was making the hurt someone else's, but even they had limits.

A moment later, they were in front of the Coven's main building, the white so blinding that Eli winced and squinted, wishing she hadn't broken her sunglasses on a previous assassination — or at least had the forethought to replace them.

"Clean your face, you look disgusting."

Eli wiped her forehead with the back of her hand. The saliva came off like flecks of rust.

Last time, Eli had stood in front of this pulsing monstrosity for hours, waiting to be let in, looking for a hidden doorway. Now, an elegant archway simply materialized in front of Circinae, and together they entered the most sacred and dangerous place in the city.

There was only one hallway. Shading her eyes, Eli followed Circinae down the hall and into a room that felt like the womb of a goddess. It was simultaneously bright and claustrophobic. It whispered of endless space and small, dirty prisons.

This effect was intentional. The architect had been the greatest witch of all time.

"You're early," said a voice that echoed against the walls. "We've only just sent the summons."

Eli smiled to herself, pleased when the timelessness of the city worked in her favour.

Slowly, as her eyes adjusted to the light, she could see the outlines of the Coven's first ring. They all wore white, creating the effect of floating heads.

Circinae knelt. Eli knelt, too.

"You bring death with you, little assassin," said another voice. Eli couldn't tell who was speaking — their mouths did not appear to move.

"I am death, lords." She responded in the usual manner.

"Then rise, so we may inspect our tool."

Eli stood, looking straight ahead. Circinae remained kneeling.

The Coven circled Eli, bits of soft fabric brushing against her skin, hands touching her hair and poking her stomach, like a doctor palpating for pain.

When the inspection was over, Circinae rose. Eli stepped back and waited for the negotiations to begin. As Circinae's daughter and a tool rather than a person, she had no say in the matter.

"We have a new target. This one must be taken out immediately. It is our utmost priority."

"So soon?" Circinae's voice dripped with honey. "She has barely rested from her last assignment, which went extremely well. I had hoped to reward her."

"She is a superior weapon," one of them conceded. "The best daughter you've ever made, Circinae. But the threat is —"

"It is not for you to question the Coven," another voice snapped, and Eli suspected they had said more than intended. "Is she ready, or does she need additional time to heal? We had thought she was a flawless design."

How many daughters had Circinae made? And what had happened to them? Eli recalled Kite's words and suppressed a shudder, questions she wished she had asked flooding her mind. *Kite, what did you discover? And what will happen to me when you are the Witch Lord, sending girls like me to their deaths or killing us yourself? Will you even call it killing?*

"Oh, she is ready, my lords," Circinae bowed again. "You have seen yourself her fitness, her expert construction. I only wanted to ensure she is handled with the care befitting a daughter of her status."

Murmuring filled the room, echoing off the smooth, gleaming walls.

"No one has denied that you have done well, Circinae. You will be rewarded for her success. Perhaps we should admit you into the third ring of the Coven, where you might better serve your people."

"I would be honoured, my lords."

Eli knew the negotiations were coming to a close. As Eli's handler, Circinae was the only person who could order Eli on missions, and so the lords had to bargain with her, granting her more power as their reliance on Eli grew.

"The details are here." A scrap of crimson velvet materialized in Eli's hand.

This was new, but Circinae took it in stride. "I will read it to you," she said, as if Eli could not read. It was a secret they kept from the Coven.

"No. This is for the weapon alone. It will speak to her mind. These secrets will only be yours when you have been inducted into the third ring."

Eli could almost feel the rage emanating from Circinae's body. It was unheard of for the Coven to give an assignment directly to an assassin.

"Very well, my lords."

The scrap of fabric twisted in her palm as Eli let it read itself to her mind, maintaining the illusion of illiteracy.

She frowned. Opened her mouth. Paused.

"May I speak, my lords?"

Circinae wheeled around and stared at her in shock and horror. Tools were forbidden from speaking in the inner sanctum of the Coven.

But tools were also forbidden from reading. Rules had already been broken. Eli felt her heart jump at this act of daring, wondering how much she would suffer for it.

"The tool may ask one question. Consider this additional payment for your services, Circinae."

Mollified at being addressed directly, Circinae nodded but shot Eli a vicious look. Her bargaining power was being halved by Eli's request.

"Where is the rest of the report? This appears incomplete."

Circinae gasped at the audacity of the question that implied error or weakness. But Eli had never received only a name before. Where were the eyelashes, the fingernail, the taste of sweat? Names could be stolen, discarded, or lost — only the signature of flesh would ensure a successful mission.

"The report is complete. Unless you are incapable of performing this task without additional information?" The voice was mild, but the question was venomous and sharp, and directed at Eli rather than her mother.

"No, my lords. This will suffice." To be safe, Eli bent into a formal bow again.

"Then you are dismissed."

Eli was sent out of the chamber while Circinae completed the negotiation.

Outside, the sky was striped purple and green, and Eli sat on the steps and stared up at the beauty of the clouds. She wanted to go back to the river, to lie down on soft moss with Kite and watch the clouds turn into fantastical creatures and ships.

The daydream ended with Circinae's arrival. Eli tensed. Her outburst had ruined Circinae's bargaining. She waited for her punishment.

To her surprise, Circinae said nothing, only stared into her daughter's crocodile eyes thoughtfully, made a soft sound to herself, and then stepped away. "You are to leave immediately," she said, looking out at the bustling city streets.

She turned back to Eli and brushed her palm against Eli's cheek. Eli froze. Circinae repeated the words she always said before a mission: "My glory is your glory.

Your victory is my victory. You are a tool and you have value. The Coven will honour us for our service."

"Your glory is my glory," said Eli dutifully. "My victory is your victory. I am a tool and I have value. The Coven will honour us for our service."

"Remember," Circinae said suddenly, her pupils like flames in the whites of her eyes, "remember that I taught you how to read."

Then she was gone. Eli was alone, the fading warmth of Circinae's hand on her cheek, a name burned into her memory:

Virginia White.

Six

Eli was unravelling.

She could feel the fear and confusion stir in her body like leaves in the fall. *His glasses askew, one arm broken* —

She had a mission. That should have been enough. It had been a long time since she felt this uncertain, and the feeling left her adrift, lonely and lost on the blinding steps. Her heart thudded in her chest.

The mission. The name. That was her mark. All she had to do was what she did best. And then she could return to her moss bed, frolic with Kite under the river, parry words and wits with Circinae, and prepare for the next job. Gather knowledge and grow strong. Increase her value.

She'd always been given time to rest before. Time to heal, to train.

She wanted a black coffee more than anything else in the worlds.

Eli shook her head and then tied her hair back. This wasn't the time for questions. *They never give you time to question*, a voice in her head reminded her. She dug her nails into her palm and took a deep breath in. Then out. *You're not a child anymore, and this isn't a fairytale. This is your life. You have accepted it.*

It was time.

Again.

Eli unfolded the glamour that Circinae had left on the steps. She must have finished knitting it while Eli was with Kite. She slid it over her skin, the magic sticky and hot. A sensation like pins and needles tingled along her limbs as she settled into it. This glamour made her appear shorter and curvier, with longer hair and dark eyes, dressed in greys and blacks. Heavy eyeliner. Goth chic. The only concession Circinae had made was keeping her glasses as they were. Eli loved her frames.

She opened her body to the universe, to the winds that blew between worlds. The shifting, glittering tunnel of dark appeared before her. She was like an ant on a giant pile of black sand. Closing her eyes, clutching the pendant that hung around her throat, Eli stepped into the heart of the wild.

Eli stumbled out of the Vortex and fell onto the cement in a heap, hair tangled and matted. It had been wilder this time, tearing at her hair and clothes, trying to shake her loose. She had almost been thrust out several times. She wondered what would have happened if it had spat her out earlier — would she have fallen up or down? Could a girl made of spiderweb and glass break like a human of flesh and bone? She felt the beginning of bruises on her knees and elbows and suspected the answer was yes.

"Are you okay?"

Eli looked up. Someone was looking down at her. They were Black with short, spiky purple hair and golden-brown eyes. Eli was stunned. She wasn't supposed to be noticed by humans.

The frost blade bit into her thigh. She winced. "Bad girl," she muttered, adjusting the hilt.

"What?" They were wearing black skinny jeans and a leather jacket. Both ears were covered in silver earrings that caught the light. Eli had a sudden urge to bite the highest ring.

"I said I'm fine." Eli stood up and wiped the dirt off her torn jeans. A hand reached over and brushed some gravel off her shoulder. Eli flinched.

"Sorry! Just trying to help." Their eyes were still watching her. Eli wondered if her lipstick was smudged or if there were vulture feathers in her hair.

"I don't need your help," Eli snapped. She should have flashed a smile, made some excuse, and walked away, but she felt off her game.

And the purple spikes reminded her of a sea urchin.

"Sorry," they repeated. They were looking at her with curiosity, eyes mapping the smudged glasses and dirty fingernails, the bruised knee and ripped jeans. Their look was electric. Eli felt the hair on her arms stand up. She wasn't used to being stared at. She was a shadow, a nightmare, death in dark corners. She was a daughter of the Coven.

"It's fine," she said. "Don't worry about it."

The thorn blade pricked through her jeans. Eli clenched her jaw.

"You hurt? You get hit by a car or something?"

"Something like that. I'm okay."

They didn't leave. They smelled like flower petals and gasoline. The spikes reminded her of home.

"Where you headed? I can give you a ride."

That's when Eli noticed the bike: a gleaming black-and-chrome motorcycle with thick, muscular wheels. Wide leather seats. The green outline of a mermaid spray-painted on the fender.

"Is that yours?" Eli wanted to touch it.

Purple Hair grinned. "Yep. And I have a spare helmet."

"Why are you offering to help me?" No one helped anyone for free. There was always a cost. Unconsciously, Eli touched the pendant that hung around her neck.

The stranger shrugged. "You seem lost. And you look familiar — did we meet at Pride last year?"

"No."

"Well, I've definitely seen you around town. I'm Tav." Tav tugged off a leather glove and held out their hand.

She shook Tav's hand. Static electricity crackled where their fingers brushed against one another. Eli's palm came away warm, a tendril of smoke curling into the air from the friction.

What was happening? Could Tav feel it, too? If they did, they didn't show it, just slid their glove back on in one fluid movement.

"I don't remember seeing you." Eli curled her hand into a fist.

"What? But I'm so memorable!" Tav threw on a look of mock horror. "Stunningly gorgeous, notorious bad boy. Or bad girl, depending on who you're asking." They winked at Eli. "This city doesn't get people like me."

"This city doesn't get people like me, either," Eli murmured, head reeling from Tav's introduction.

"I kind of figured. You seem like a bit of a loner."

"I'm shy."

Tav raised an eyebrow. "You don't seem shy. Pissed off, maybe."

"I'm not interested in making friends."

Eli wondered why she was being so honest. It was true: she was often lonely, but her brief visits to the human world were always for reconnaissance, training, or assassination. It would never be her home, so why try? Witch tools didn't have friends.

Circinae had often disciplined her for not doing a better job cultivating a network of human contacts she could exploit to do her job. But Eli worked best alone, and she didn't need any humans hanging around asking questions or reminding her that she didn't belong. Instead, she'd worked on becoming a shadow, on slipping in and out of rooms and crowds unnoticed. She'd practised using her knives. She told herself these were the skills that mattered.

Besides, she had Kite. That had to be enough. Once she had wanted —

But she was older now. She understood her place.

"That's too bad. Think of all the rides you missed out on."

Tav was smiling at her. The sun glinted off the black helmet cradled in their arm. Eli felt her heart move strangely, like a fish newly released into the ocean. The light caught the hilt of the frost blade and burst across her vision. Eli wondered if the blade was as excited as she was, or if it knew something she didn't.

In a moment of human spontaneity, Eli did the first truly rebellious thing she had ever done: she decided to trust them.

"Guess we should start making up for it then."

Tav blinked in surprise and then laughed. "I agree completely. Here." They handed Eli their spare helmet. "Safety first."

The idea of being safe was so absurd to Eli that she started laughing and couldn't stop, even as she snapped on her helmet and climbed up behind Tav.

"Crazy girl," said Tav. It sounded like a compliment. "Where are we going?"

Her cold thighs against Tav's warm body. The smell of metal and dish soap and peonies. Eli's heart was racing dangerously fast, and she wondered if this was better than the thrill of the hunt or the burn of caffeine.

"Anywhere," said Eli.

Tav revved the engine, and they tore off down the city streets.

Seven

Tav drove clear through town and stopped at a café Eli had never seen before. It was called The Sun. It was a grand name for an unassuming hovel, the sign hand-painted and faded with age.

"Best coffee in the city," said Tav.

Eli said nothing, still exhilarated by the rush of wind on her face and the simmering panic of running away from her life. For a moment, she couldn't breathe.

"Need help?" Tav offered a hand, but Eli, already feeling in their debt, swung herself off the bike gracefully. She made herself breathe again.

Tav raised an eyebrow appreciatively. Eli had to smother a smile. She spent so much time obsessing over what her body was made from that she often forgot how well it moved. She wasn't used to being admired. It felt dangerous.

Eli liked danger.

"Thanks for the ride. Smoother than it looks."

"First time?" Tav sounded surprised. "You didn't seem nervous at all."

"I don't get nervous." She wasn't bragging — it was the truth.

"Another hole in your 'shy' story."

Before Eli could think of an appropriate response, Tav had turned and walked inside. A bell tinkled faintly as they entered. Eli smelled rose petals and sage. It reminded her of the apothecary Circinae used to take her to when she was little. No one told her what had happened to him. People vanished in the witches' city all the time — not always by choice, but often enough that she had never been too worried when an acquaintance disappeared for a month or a year.

Then again, magic ran on sacrifice, and the world sometimes took what it was owed.

"Large Americano and whatever my friend wants," Tav told the barista, leaning on the counter. "God, I love your necklace."

The woman behind the counter blushed and stammered a "thank you."

Were they friends? Is that what Eli wanted?

"Large coffee. Black." Eli unconsciously stepped into a patch of shadow and leaned against the cracked wooden wall. The barista slid a large mug across the counter.

"Grab us a seat," said Tav. "I'll find you."

Eli should have downed the coffee, turned around, and marched out the door. Returned to her mission. Instead, she found herself taking the mug, shrugging, and then sitting down at a table in one corner.

The sun streamed in through the windows. Eli felt very visible. It was strange. She wasn't used to being looked at the way Tav looked at her — like she was a person, like she was more than a witch's tool. She wondered if that reflected poorly on her training. Did she stand out when she was supposed to blend in?

But she liked it.

Tav was still flirting cheerfully with the barista. Eli surreptitiously inspected her palm. It was unblemished, but the scent of smoke lingered. Frowning, she placed it back on her knee under the table. She sipped the coffee, wincing as the heat burned her lips, and watched Tav's purple spikes catch the light, turning violet and lavender and royal blue. Before long, Tav was in front of Eli, all eyes and leather and smiles.

"Thanks again." Eli kept reaching for words and watching them slip through her fingers. She shouldn't be here. Strangely, she didn't feel anxious. Her heart was beating smoothly, her breathing even and calm. She felt more relaxed than she had in years. Not dream-lulled, like she sometimes felt with Kite, but the kind of calm that comes with warm sunshine on a Sunday morning.

"Nice to have the company."

A pause.

"I like your name," Eli offered.

"Thanks. Picked it myself." Tav winked.

"Where's it from?"

"I read *Dawn* like a million times. Just one of those books that sticks with you, you know?"

"*Dawn*?"

"Humanity's almost been destroyed by nuclear war? The main character mates with an alien — well, kind of. And the aliens have three genders?"

Eli shook her head. "Never heard of it."

"Dude. You need to fix that immediately. Octavia Butler is amazing."

"Yes, sir," said Eli, arching an eyebrow.

"Thank god. My good deed for the day is done." Tav took a sip and then sighed. "Best. Damn. Coffee. Ever."

Eli was about halfway through hers and still hadn't felt the angry kick of caffeine that would jolt her into action. She felt at peace.

"What is this place? It's … different."

Tav studied her face intently before answering. "I don't know," they said. "But something about it always brings me back, even though it's never on my way. It just feels … right."

Eli nodded. She could feel it, too. "Why did you bring me here?"

Tav looked away, a slight frown wrinkling the skin around their eyes. "I don't know exactly. Finding you like that — like you'd walked out of a storm, or maybe a story — and you were crackling with this kind of energy. I just knew you needed to be here."

"What kind of energy? Do you see auras or something?" Eli had met some of the new age types who played
with fortune-telling and rituals. She had always laughed
at them before, but maybe humans had their own kind
of magic.

"Something like that. Yeah. And yours was … wild.
Like nothing I'd ever seen before."

"Is that a pick-up line?" Eli found herself smiling.

Tav laughed. "Hey, it usually works like a charm."

"I'll bet." Eli rolled her eyes. Her gaze snagged on
a succulent on the bar, its leaves writhing wildly. She
blinked, and the plant was static again. Ordinary.

"Any time I get tired of driving around town, feeling stuck and tired and frustrated, I come here," Tav said,
dragging Eli's attention back to them. "And then I feel a
bit better. I sound crazy, I know."

"No." Eli caught their eye. "No, you don't. I feel it, too."

Tav leaned back and stretched. "I wish I could stay
here all day. Forget about the world."

"No." Eli played with the handle of the mug. "You'd
get bored."

"True."

There was a pause as they both finished their drinks.

"There's one more thing I'd like to show you," said
Tav, looking out the window. "Will you come with me?"

"Okay," said Eli, surprised by how much she wanted to.

Eli enjoyed the second ride better. She could feel the
sun on her shoulders, the warm leather on her thighs.
She watched Tav's body moving with the rhythm of their

breathing. The wind in her face was warm, tossing up dirt and gravel and dead insects.

Tav stopped at a hill just past the city limits. It was a rocky outcropping looking over the river. Eli had never come here. It was too far away from the heart of the town, where ghosts stalked prey and assassins stalked ghosts.

Tav clambered over the rocks carelessly and Eli followed, trying to remember to scuff her feet or kick stray pebbles. She didn't need to show off.

(She wanted to show off.)

The sky was beginning to darken. Eli had never figured out how time worked between the worlds. But it was late afternoon at least — she could see the sun thinning like a worn-out blouse, and night coming into view behind it.

"This way." Tav's hand grabbed hers. Eli was grateful for the leather gloves that kept their skin from touching. She wanted to feel Tav's skin against hers. She knew these thoughts were dangerous.

They led Eli over the jumbled rocks until they arrived at a large slab of granite. Eli felt a sense of camaraderie with the rock. When her feet scraped the stone, it rang out with a tone that resonated deep in her bones. Granite.

Tav sat down, cross-legged, and pulled their gloves off, stretching their fingers. Eli followed more cautiously, slowly lowering herself onto the surface.

All of Eli's blades began vibrating, sending tremors of energy down both of her femurs. Eli wondered what they wanted. *To cut.*

"This is the most magical view in the city." Tav's breath tickled Eli's ear. Eli closed her eyes and felt warmth radiating off the human body beside her. Breathed in the scent of leather and oil. Shivered.

"Eli. Open your eyes."

Eli did. She looked out over the simple human world. A thin grey stripe of river twisted below their feet. Iron-black trees, bark peeling off like old skin, stabbed angrily at the horizon. And behind the veil of day, the moon was coming home. It glowed, ghostly and fantastical, a giant white orb that seemed to take up most of the sky.

It was breathtaking.

"How did you find this place?" Eli asked. Even after all her years coming to the City of Ghosts, there were many places she had never seen.

Tav chewed their lip for a second before answering. "I was looking for someone. Something, maybe." They glanced furtively at Eli, who kept her face impassive. "I stole my mom's bike and took it for a joyride. After that, she told me to get my damn licence." Tav laughed. Fondness had spilled into their tone like nutmeg.

"Where is she now?" asked Eli.

"Home." Their voice slammed shut like a window. "I moved out."

The granite block caught the light and reflected it back to the sky. Eli looked into Tav's eyes and saw her own reflection in them. Heavy bangs, dirty glasses —

"They're not contacts, are they?"

"What?" Eli drew back. Her glamour was still in place. Tav should not be able to see her true form. Narrow reptilian eyes that never blinked bore into Tav, daring them to run.

What would she do if they ran? Could she let them live?

"Your eyes." Tav's voice was low. It hummed through Eli's body and she knew in that moment she could not kill them, not now, not here. She couldn't leave Tav an orange smear on this rock.

"It's okay. I'm not scared." Tav leaned closer. Eli felt her heart racing at their proximity. She could see the gold flecks in their dark eyes and the brown roots of their hair.

Her blades hungered for death.

"No!" In a flash, Eli pushed Tav away from her. Snatching the keys from Tav's pocket, Eli jumped up and ran. Heart pounding, adrenalin pumping, thinking, *What did I do? What just happened?*

"Eli! Wait! Where are you going?! Eli!"

Tav's shouts chased Eli over the rocky plateau. She was going to be unmade. She had let herself be discovered by a human. If Circinae found out —

She wouldn't find out. Eli would do as she was told. Stop asking questions. Stop getting into trouble. *You are a weapon*, she thought. *You have value. Glory. Honour.*

Eli threw herself clumsily onto the bike. Shaking hands jammed the keys into place. She had to get out of here. She had a job to do. Thinking she could be free of magic by taking a joyride? Pretending she could throw off her origins and play human forever? She was still a foolish child who believed in happy endings. There was no way to avoid her fate.

But she still had human weakness in her, and so she looked back. Just once. She could see the silhouette of a person holding a motorcycle helmet in one hand. They were facing her. Not running, not shouting. Just standing, staring straight at her. And the last thing she saw before she gunned the engine was the look of hurt and accusation in Tav's eyes as they met Eli's.

They'll get over it, thought Eli.

She almost believed it.

Then she was gone, driving recklessly into the night, trying to find her way back to something that made sense. Something familiar. Something that would remind her who she was.

She had to kill someone.

Eight

The first time Eli killed a ghost, she had been welcomed back into the Children's Lair with dollar-store balloons and wildfire and the insistent claws of other children.

They were proud of her.

Like human children in the City of Ghosts, witch children in the City of Eyes were not innocent creatures to be kept pure and unstained like a silk pillowcase. They were grubby, dirty, bloodthirsty animals, vicious and feral. From the bullies on the playground that drew blood with their words to the magic girls who vivisected animals and stole power from the dead — they really weren't all that different.

You didn't earn adulthood by killing. You earned your place in the world as an assassin. You had value.

"Eli!"

"Eli's back!"

"The Stick Girl returns!"

Eli played in the mud with the other children, her hair coated with pungent wet earth.

"Ghost slayer!"

"Sister hero!"

Hands captured her wrists and spun her around. Other hands shoved berries into her face. Happily, she'd opened her mouth and swallowed. The juice was sticky and sour and made all the colours around her brighten, as if the lights had been turned up. The children had worn bright reds and blues and violets, and Christmas lights had been strung across the stone sanctuary.

Eli found herself flung outside the circle of fiercely dancing bodies. She was caught by damp arms and heard a familiar voice in her ear.

"You have returned to us, little sister," the purr echoed in Eli's head. She turned, still encircled by Kite's arms. Daringly, she pressed her forehead against Kite's. Surprisingly, the witch child's skin was warm. "The Warlord must have been watching over you."

The Warlord: a myth, a legend, a god. An invisible friend to keep you company when you were lonely, a guardian angel to watch over you, a monster under the bed.

"Of course I came back. You need me."

Kite laughed. "To keep me out of trouble?"

"To help you get into it." Her yellow eyes glittered dangerously.

"You are our champion now, ghost killer, toy assassin. The children were afraid you would die in the human world."

"Sticks can't die," Eli retorted.

"But they can break." Kite's hair floated around her head as if she was submerged in water. Strands brushed against Eli's face. She closed her eyes and let them pet her gently, insistently.

"You are stained with death now. You are one of us."

The pure joy Eli felt at that pronouncement was unimaginable, dissolving on her tongue like sugar. Sweet and potent. *One of us.*

She opened her eyes. Kite's pupil-less gaze stared back. Kite smiled widely and leaned closer. Eli's breath caught. She found herself staring at Kite's lips, blue like frostbitten leaves.

Kite's tongue darted out and licked the corner of Eli's mouth.

Eli gasped at the sensation. She closed her eyes and leaned in further, her mouth opening.

Kite's teeth closed around Eli's lower lip. She bit down. Eli cried out. Kite pulled back, a blush spreading across her cheeks. Blood mixed with the berry juice on both of their mouths, dripping over their chins.

"Blood keeps us together," whispered Kite. Eli nodded.

Kite had pushed her back into the revelry and vanished. The lights and sound and touch swallowed Eli into a whirlwind of chaos and life.

Where had Kite gone when she'd disappeared from the children's celebrations? When she could not be found for weeks and weeks, and Eli had missed her so desperately it hurt? Why was Kite always at the edges of the play?

Eli would not have the answers to these questions for some time.

Nine

Eli drove quickly, circling closer and closer to the heart of the city. She was a hawk hunting her prey.

This knowledge soothed her wicked heart.

She ditched the bike on a narrow side street. She didn't have much time before Tav came for it — especially if they had tracking activated on their phone. Humans were so easy to steal from. Tav hadn't even noticed Eli slip her hand in their jacket at the café. Maybe that would teach them to stop trusting strangers. Sliding off of the leather seat, Eli pulled the iPhone out of her pocket and prayed Tav had a good data plan.

Of course they did. All the kids did these days — at least, the ones who could afford motorcycles. Tav was playing bad, wearing the trappings of rebellion. Eli had seen lots of people like that, who thought ink tattoos

were permanent and spiked collars made them dangerous. They'd never experienced real danger; or, if they had,
they wouldn't have recognized it. Humans couldn't sense
ghosts, which is why it was up to witches to track these
traces of wild magic before they fed on every living thing
and upset the delicate balance between worlds.

Tav was nothing special. Just a spoiled kid with a toy,
pretending to be a soldier. That's what Eli told herself as
she pushed the image of Tav's wounded face out of her
mind's eye. *Focus on the job.*

She wondered how close Tav was to catching her. The
thrill of being chased heightened her senses, making her
a better predator.

She typed in "Virginia White" and the internet spat
out an address. Somewhere in the suburbs: unusual for a
ghost to go that far from the busy downtown streets but
not unheard of. Possibly this one was new and hadn't yet
migrated to the city centre.

*Unless it's old and powerful — smart enough to hide
from the hunters.*

She shook her head, trying to lose the thought. Her
mind was a snow globe with memories and worries and
desires drifting haphazardly.

She checked the glamour that Circinae had cast on
her knives. Usually Eli got Kite to check it, to reinforce
the enchantment when it started to tear, but she hadn't
remembered this time. She'd been too angry. Hopefully
it would last long enough for her to finish the job
undetected.

Kite. The echo of the last words Eli had spoken to her rang in her ears, and a twinge of guilt flicked up Eli's spine. *Go back to your people and leave me alone.*

She shoved the guilt away. Kite had made her decision. She'd made it that day she hadn't come, when she'd left Eli waiting alone on the island. When she pretended that all of their escape plans had been child's play. A game.

Kite had left the Children's Lair and joined the Coven. Told Eli nothing would change, but she'd lied. Everything was different now. She rarely saw Kite, and when the Heir became the Witch Lord, they would not even have those brief moments together.

Kite had a choice, and she'd chosen the witches. Chosen *wrong.*

No, she'd been right. They had both needed to grow up. *The scuffed loafer falling off a limp foot.*

Murderer.

Eli forced her painful memories away, frustrated at her spiralling thoughts. *Do the job.*

She ordered an Uber to take her to the suburbs, then tossed the phone into the street. Her own face stared back at her in the cracked glass, split into pieces. Reluctantly, she said goodbye to the bike and headed to the restaurant where she'd ordered the car. Pick-ups in back alleys always looked suspicious.

The car pulled up: white, dirty, and inconspicuous. Perfect. Eli climbed in.

"How's your night going?" asked the driver, an East Asian man with a French-villain-meets-hipster moustache. He looked to be around her age. Eli tried not to stare at his moustache.

"Not great."

"Sorry to hear that."

Eli shrugged. "It's fine. Just … work stuff."

"Bad day?"

"Coworker drama."

"That's the worst."

"Yeah."

"What are you up tonight? Something more fun?"

"Not really. Visiting a colleague. A different one. It's a work thing. Dinner."

"Early dinner," he commented. Eli felt a surge of anger at his inane questions, and her inability to answer them.

"Her kids have soccer practice later."

"Ah."

They drove in silence for a while, and Eli had to stop herself from tapping her fingernails on the window anxiously. She wanted this over with.

He pulled up outside the address Eli had given him — a few houses away from the hit. "Be careful," he told her.

"At dinner?"

He played with his moustache. "You want me to wait for you? Ubers don't always want to come out this far. Might be hard to get a ride back."

Eli felt a spike of worry. "What are you saying?" Her hand curled around the door handle, ready to run.

"I'm saying humans aren't entirely useless. Some of us are hired to help, okay?"

Reeling with the implications — Who had hired him? How did he know who she was? — Eli managed to snap back, "You leave a car here and the cops will find us immediately. So, no, you're not helping."

"Find someone who isn't an Uber driver? Driving a car he doesn't own? They can try." He smiled and tapped a thumb against the steering wheel. "You'd better get going. I guess I won't be here to take you back then. You're on your own from here."

"I'm always on my own. And I don't need your help."

"What makes you so sure those things are true?" He raised an eyebrow, obviously pleased to have knowledge that an assassin didn't. The arrogance of humans never failed to amaze and exasperate her.

Grunting in response, Eli pulled the handle and then kicked the door open viciously. The metal of the car groaned, threatening to come apart.

"Careful!"

"Why do you care? I thought it wasn't your car."

He made eye contact for the first time, and when he spoke, the confidence had drained from his voice. "I've never met one like you before."

"Deadly *and* a great sense of humour?"

"You just seem so ... human."

Eli didn't respond to that, just slid out of the car and closed the door silently to make up for her temper tantrum.

He rolled down the window. "Good luck."

"I don't need luck," she said. "I'll see you soon."

He laughed like she was joking, but she wasn't. He had answers, and she was going to hunt him down and get them.

She already had his scent and the pattern of his heartbeat. Foolish human.

Ten

The house was quiet. A gentle wind picked up the arms of the poplar tree and brushed them across the shutters lovingly. The porch light was off. Everything was shadows and whispers. Eli felt her shoulders relax. She closed her eyes. She took a deep breath in and tasted laundry detergent, instant coffee, dried blood.

The moment before the dance. *This* was where she belonged.

She was never more herself than when she was hunting.

She didn't catch the scent that most ghosts carried. But an experienced ghost, a ghost that had fed on human and witch alike — that ghost might have taken in the essence of the house and its occupants. Ghosts were a bit like sponges that way. This one was old, and clever. Eli felt her pulse quicken in anticipation. Finally, a worthy opponent. It had been so long.

In the dark, there were no lovers or enemies, no heartsick girls with seashells in their hair, no regrets or childish fantasies of freedom. There was only here and now, and the promise of death.

Eli flowed between the darkest shadows on the lawn. She skirted around the front porch with the automatic light and the peepholes and windows that could betray her presence.

She picked the attic window.

All right, she was showing off. She wanted to stand over the house and look down over the world that was always above her.

She wanted to feel like a god.

Silently, she scaled the wall. It was easy. She was strong. The attic window was round and crusted with mould. Eli took out the pearl blade. Although it was designed to separate magic from non-magic, in the human world it could be coaxed to tear apart many different materials. She pressed it against the windowpane and the blade performed its alchemy, turning glass back into sand and sodium carbonate and limestone. The window crumbled.

Eli entered the home.

"Come out, come out, wherever you are," she whispered, grinning at her own joke.

She thought, *I am the monster under the bed*. She smiled wider, the glamour struggling to keep up with her crocodile teeth. She didn't need to conceal her true form now.

The house was silent. She padded gently across the floor. Down the stairs. She trailed her finger along the narrow railing that curved and twisted away from her like a snake. But no one escaped her blades.

Next, the bedroom: rustling sheets, a soft gasp like a baby's cry, a crackle of old springs. This would be the sacred place of death. This is where she would fulfill her purpose and keep both worlds safe. Her shoulders straightened with the weight of this calling. Her vocation. Invisible, brutal, and unloved — but necessary. Sometimes that was enough. *You have value.*

The figure didn't wake as Eli hovered over it. She had to be sure. She leaned down, drawing the thorn blade, and pricked the bottom of a foot. Ghosts bled smoke or iron or scales. Once she had killed a ghost that had burst into a cloud of floral perfume.

A single drop of red blood beaded at the cut.

Ghosts didn't bleed red.

The body woke up screaming. Eli threw a hand over the woman's mouth to stifle the sound, mind racing.

"What's your name?" demanded Eli. "Stop screaming and I won't hurt you." She slowly took her hand away from the woman's mouth.

"Take anything you want. My wallet is in the drawer. Please take anything, just don't hurt me."

Impatient and flustered by the ghost's response, Eli grabbed her hair and forced their faces together. "I asked for your name."

"J-Jennifer White," she stuttered. "What do you want?"

"No," said Eli angrily. "It's Virginia. This house belongs to Virginia."

A look of confusion crossed the woman's face.

"My mother's dead," she whispered. "She died last year."

"How did she die?"

"Stroke."

Eli released her head. The woman scrambled back. Eli reached for the frost blade. It burned like ice at her touch. Her blades never lied.

The woman was telling the truth.

"You're human," said Eli.

"Of course I'm human!" The woman looked at Eli. "Are you on drugs? I can call an ambulance."

She had the wrong person.

She had made a mistake.

Eli stumbled back. "I'm sorry." She fumbled at her waist, sheathing the daggers. The woman took the opportunity to lunge at Eli with a large pillow. The pillow snagged on the thorn dagger, knocking Eli back and tossing a handful of feathers into the air. They fell like snow.

The woman ran for the door. Eli knew she should kill her. Had she seen the sharp teeth through the fading glamour? Had crocodile eyes burned through the enchanted mask?

Instead, Eli stood in a cloud of feathers and watched her go.

She was not made to kill humans. There was no glory or honour in it.

Knowing the police would be here in a matter of minutes, she dragged herself back up to the attic and scrambled through the empty eye socket of the house.

My existence is marked by empty spaces, she thought bitterly.

The sound of sirens in the distance.

She ran.

Eleven

Eli ran wildly, her footsteps on asphalt echoing through the quiet street. She struggled to keep her glamour in place. Her heart was beating out of her rib cage. She turned left, then right, then right again, randomly, spurred on by panic.

A dead end.

The sirens were getting closer. Should she break into another house? Try to outrun the cars? She looked around for somewhere to hide.

A black car flashed its headlights at her, and she jumped back, grabbing two of her knives — one made from rose thorns, the other carved from stone.

The window rolled down and a familiar head poked out. "Need a lift?"

"What the fuck are you doing here?"

"Heard the call. I listen in on cop activity. Lots of times it's witch crap."

Eli slid over the hood of the car, wrenched open the passenger door, and fell into the seat.

He grinned. "What were you saying about not needing me?"

"Yes, you're very useful for a human. Now get me the hell out of here."

"What's the magic word?"

"I was trained to kill?"

"Good enough for me." He put the car into gear and drove off.

Alto saxophone drifted from the speakers.

Eli nearly dropped her weapons. "This is your getaway music?"

"I like jazz. What's wrong with jazz?"

Eli shrugged and sheathed her blades. "Can you go any faster?"

"I could, but then the cops would chase me. Gotta blend in." He glanced over at her. "Everything okay?"

"I don't want to talk about it."

"What happened?"

"What did I just say?"

He drove under the speed limit. He stopped at stop signs. He yielded right of way. It was painful. She threw him an exasperated look when he stopped at a yellow light.

"What?"

"Nothing." She slouched down into the seat, trying to calm her heartbeat. "Nice moustache."

"Thank you."

"Ever heard of sarcasm?"

"Is that a fun place to visit?"

Eli rolled her eyes.

"I'm Cam," he said.

She didn't answer. They drove in silence for a few minutes.

"Do you want me to drop you off downtown?"

She hesitated.

"Or somewhere else?" He sounded nervous. She didn't blame him.

"Downtown," she said. "I have to go back and report in." The thought filled her with dread, a slow poison in her stomach. She didn't want to go back. Failure was not tolerated. But she had nowhere else to go.

"Okay."

He pulled up outside City Hall, a building so like and yet unlike the Coven. Tall and imposing, built to withstand storms and centuries. But somehow empty and dead, where the Coven was alive.

She hesitated. Took a breath. Prepared to face her punishment.

"If you need anything, I'm here to help."

"Says the hired hand."

"Well, I do get paid." He shrugged. "But that's not why I do this. Mercenaries don't last long in my position. I *want* to help."

"I already said I don't need help."

He didn't say anything.

"Okay. I'm going." She opened the door and climbed out. She hesitated. "Thanks, Cam." Then, her hand still on the door, "I'm Eli."

He gave her privacy to do the dirty business of summoning a hole between worlds.

Twelve

Eli closed her eyes and stretched out her arms. She felt for the lining of the world, where the fabric thinned, where she could move from the human realm to where the witches ruled. She fumbled for the seam.

All she felt was smooth sky and sparks of magic like electricity tickling and teasing her fingertips. She frowned, reached farther, sent her mind out. Stretched her thorn-and-flesh body to the land of its birth.

I am one of yours, she told the magic world in the sky. *Come for me. Please take me home. Take me away from here.*

She wondered how long it would take the cops to find her.

She wondered if going back was a mistake.

She wondered if there were other human operatives watching her right now.

She wondered if *she* was a mistake.

No. Keep your concentration.

She took a breath. *There!*

The seam split, an opening in time and space. Finally, she was in the Vortex, surrounded by silence. Taking her away from motorcycles and madness, and a boi with eyes like liquid gold. Taking her home, where the rules were chaos and power, everything lived and breathed magic, and the exchange of knowledge was everything. There, Eli knew what she was worth, and she could bargain. She had a place and a purpose.

Didn't she?

Was that enough?

In the human city, she was no one. A lost girl with desires and needs that had nothing to do with calculation and planning. Jazz and leather jackets couldn't save her. Maybe she hadn't chosen this life, but it was hers. Eli would leave the dreaming girl behind.

The Vortex froze.

Eli was suspended, caught between worlds. Hanging like a fly in a web. Held up with strands of magic.

She was nowhere.

Terror rattled her heart. Eli tried to turn her head and realized she was frozen in a block of black ice. All she could see was the darkness, but it had solidified and trapped her inside it.

Time seemed to stop. Eli couldn't tell if only a minute had passed or an hour. She didn't know how the two worlds were aligned. What if she was stuck here while a generation passed? Would she return to find Kite gone forever, just a floating voice in a white chamber? Would she have a home? She thought of Tav and Cam. Would they wonder what happened to the girl with crocodile eyes, tell stories about her to their grandchildren? And would she be the hero or villain of the story, or just a monster used to frighten toddlers into good behaviour?

Why had she been created? Was it truly to hunt down ghosts, to protect the human world, and to keep the witches' world a secret, as she had been told?

Was her entire existence a lie?

A much younger Eli had thought herself a vigilante superhero, protecting the human citizens from the haunted echoes of witch blood, the sinister and sneaky souls who had crossed the forbidden boundary. Those creatures had used their last magic on a human-like glamour, hunting prey of flesh and blood to feed their existence and replenish their disguise.

Now she was less sure.

Tears filled her eyes and froze. Everything was black ice.

Eli was going to die in this magic coffin.

After what felt like hours, Eli heard a new sound, like metal being torn apart. Again, she tried to move, but her muscles were trapped. Through the ice, she saw a bright turquoise light, pulsing faintly. It reminded her of an iridescent jellyfish in the ocean.

She smelled saltwater and knew that Kite had come for her.

Eli had never seen Kite's true form. Witches were pure magic pushed into bodies to meet the demands of the world they were in. Eli had long suspected the world they now occupied wasn't their original home — or was only one of many.

Kite's formless light was so beautiful that Eli wanted to cry. As Kite floated nearer, moving through the darkness, Eli saw tendrils of light reaching through the ice toward her. She realized she could shift slightly, that the solid block was melting. She reached out, her hand trembling, toward the essence that was her best friend.

Suddenly, another smell blocked out the familiar seaside aroma of Kite's skin. Burnt sugar. Cigarette. Lavender with an undertone of cinnamon. Kite's essence recoiled and Eli's hand froze reaching outward, grasping for something, anything.

Another essence moved, stuttering and sparking through the darkness, a redorange flame like Mars moving through the galaxy —

Circinae.

With a shriek, the blue planet threw itself at the red. The two shapes danced and fought brilliantly, fiercely, folding over one another in an intricate pattern, leaving sunspots on Eli's eyes until she couldn't see the battle.

Had they come to save her or to kill her? Had they come alone, or had the Coven sent them? Which one was the killer and which one the saviour?

Circinae and Kite fought tirelessly over the suspended girl drifting out into the cosmos in a block of ice.

They fought like gods, their magic sometimes shaping itself into great swords and spears only to collapse into the other body and re-form into its home sun.

Eli didn't know whom she wanted to win. Her mother was selfish and, like all witches, valued power and purpose over sentiment. But Kite, too, was growing into her destiny. Each had strong ties to the Coven. Each, in their own way, loved her.

On the edge of the universe, the only two people Eli cared about hurled themselves at each other again and again.

A crack of thunder shook Eli's tomb as great arms of blue lightning split through the red mass. With a sigh of pain, the red faded, receding into the black. In an instant, Kite's essence was back, cutting through the ice.

Eli was free.

A tendril of light reached out. *Take my hand*, said Kite's voice — only deeper and richer, like the sound of a shell held to an ear. An ocean sighing over the mortal body.

Eli saw again, in her mind's eye, the glorious rust-orange planet going dark. She looked into Kite's essence and saw nothing of her friend, only a magic core that glowed as bright as the Coven.

She flinched away from the beating heart of raw power.

In that moment, the dark behind Kite turned cloudy and red, like a sandstorm. It swept over Kite and Eli and turned everything to pink dust. Circinae's voice filled her head — *Finish what you started, daughter* — and then the essence of her mother pushed Eli forcibly back into the human world.

She hit the ground hard, cracking her head on the asphalt.

The Vortex was closed. Only the stale taste of old magic in Eli's mouth convinced her that what she had witnessed was real. She stood, wincing, and held a hand to the back of her head, where a cut was leaking sticky blood, smelling of iron and fear.

Where was Kite? Had Circinae killed her?

Eli didn't know. But she was going to get answers.

Thirteen

This time, it was a mint-green minivan with a licence plate that read FXYLDY.

"I thought you were trying to blend in."

"Minivans are the epitome of blending in. And I didn't have a lot of notice."

"How did you know I was still here?" Eli hadn't even tried to track him down. He had just appeared. Again.

"Tracked you."

"How? Your tech doesn't work with magic."

"It *was* magic," he said. "I'm not an idiot."

Eli sighed and turned down the jazz. "I need your help."

"I knew it!" He flung one arm around her shoulders. "What can I do for you?"

"I'm looking for someone. I just need a phone and a ride."

"Name?" He retrieved his arm and pulled out his phone. "I'm a Google master."

"No."

"You just said you wanted my help."

"You want to be an accomplice to murder? I'm not telling you anything. Give me the phone."

What if this mark was also a human? Why would the Coven want a human dead? For the first time in years, Eli was curious. And curious young women are dangerous — especially when heavily armed.

"You make a good point." He glanced sideways at her. "You don't seem that happy about it yourself."

Eli slumped down in her seat. Rain had begun to fall, and the scratching of the windshield wipers was giving her a headache. Did Circinae know what was going on? Could she get her mother to tell her? Unlikely.

"If I fail, do you turn me over to the Coven?"

He kept his tone neutral. "You failed?"

"No! I mean, not yet. I just wondered. Is it your job to make sure we don't run?"

Running? That had never been an option.

Finish what you started, daughter.

Cam was shaking his head. "No one would trust a human to go after a ghost assassin."

"But they gave you magic."

Cam didn't say anything. Mournful trombone spilled out of the speakers.

He drummed his hands on the steering wheel. "Do you trust me?"

"No."

He sighed. "If I show you something, will you promise not to kill anyone?"

Eli held her hands up as if to say, *See, unarmed?*

"You have knives all over your body."

"I won't kill anyone I don't have to."

"I'm guessing that's the closest to a promise I'll get."

"Yep."

"You want answers?" He turned the music back up and then had to shout over it. "You've come to the right guy!" FXYLDY took to the streets.

"Where are we going?!"

Cam grinned. "Headquarters! But first, my place. You need a shower — and you're bleeding all over my minivan."

Eli had to admit she felt better with clean hair and dry clothes. She had showered with her knives within arm's reach. She still didn't trust Cam, although he hadn't tried to kill her yet, and in her line of work, that was something.

He made her feel like more than a weapon.

"My roommate's out for the night," he'd said. "No one's going to bother us."

After she got dressed, she wrapped her hair up in a towel and explored the apartment. She'd never had the luxury of just looking at a human's home; she was always on a mission. It was the attic of a house, with a slanted roof and a window ledge to sit on. Everything was covered in books: the ledge, the small table, the sofa, the floor. Stacks of books everywhere. Then there were the bookcases, which took up most of the space.

"You really like cowboy erotica."

"You want to borrow? I'd recommend *Studs in Spurs*, one through seven. Number eight sucked."

"Maybe next time."

"You ready?"

No. She wanted more time to understand how Cam lived, to impress in her memory an image of the two-bedroom apartment that meant freedom, to pick up these books and read openly without the fear of being caught. To choose how to spend her days …

If she couldn't trust in her purpose, then who was she? Was she even allowed to ask?

"To meet your little gang of friends? Sure. But this time I get to drive."

Cam groaned.

The rain was falling harder now, transforming street-lamps and neon signs into stars and comets. The wind-shield wipers scraped across the glass. Eli had a million questions, but she had learned when to stay silent. When to wait and to listen.

Eli drove. Cam gave her directions.

"We're here. Pull over anywhere."

She stopped. Cam got out of the car. After a moment, Eli followed.

They were standing outside The Sun.

During the day, the sleepy café had been a hipster's dream, with round windows and exposed brick, natural sunlight, and succulents dotting the windowsills. It was different at night. The brick was shiny and dark, like volcanic glass. The handle of the door and the shutters and rooftop were curved and wicked and sharp, like a toothy animal that might bite. It looked like a witch's house.

They approached the door. A chime sounded, and a mirror appeared in a rippling motion across the surface. Cam leaned in and breathed on the glass. The fog of his breath hung in the air for a moment, clouding the door. Then it swung open.

"Deadly assassins first." Cam winked and gestured for Eli to enter. Inside, the café looked the same, cute and cozy, sleepy and somehow intoxicating. Eli felt like she had been drinking. Her head was clouded, and her body felt relaxed. Her glamour unravelled like a long silk scarf and left her not-quite-human body visible to everyone in the room.

Eli shook the enchantment out of her head. She was sharp edges again, but she could feel the magic — subtle, like a single fennel leaf in soup — prodding at her consciousness, trying to lull her, trick her, catch her. Switching to her all-black magic set of eyes, she could see a thread of blue light snaking its way around her elbow. She pinched it between thumb and forefinger and threw it back into one corner. It curled in on itself like a dejected animal.

"Oh, she's good," a deep voice declared. Eli glanced up at a woman with a thin line for a mouth and a calculating gaze, then blinked away her dark eyes for the familiar crocodile yellow. There was so much magic in this place that she couldn't tell who the source was, and the swirling colours and lights were giving her a migraine. She didn't bother to pick up the scraps of her disguise — the magic in this place was too strong. Besides, it was time these humans knew who — and *what* — they were dealing with.

"Eli." She offered a hand, fingernails somewhere between bird talons and the ragged nails of teenagers, complete with chipped and fading blue nail polish. "It's nice to meet you."

Without taking her eyes from Eli, the woman took her hand and shook it. "Welcome, Eli. We've waited a long time."

Eli could hear the murmur of other voices, and bodies slowly materialized into her field of vision.

"Good job, Cam!"

"Missed you, Cam."

"Cam the Man!"

"Did you see any witches?"

"Did the cops stop you? I heard they were stopping everyone."

"Great work, Cameron."

"I'm the one who found her," said a familiar voice. "Don't I get any credit?"

Eli froze. Turned her head and found that challenging stare. Remembered the heat of leather on her body. Felt her fingers twitch toward her blades, drawn by instinct. Immediately retreated into shame and horror.

"Find your bike yet?" asked Eli coolly. "I'd be hurt if someone picked it up who doesn't appreciate it."

"Yeah, we found it."

Eli looked for a trace of reproach in Tav's face and saw nothing. It was a blank page.

So they'd both lied. She took a step back from the crowd. What had Tav told them about her? She had heard of witches using the bodies of former assassins or pets for all kinds of back-alley magics.

She had walked right into a trap.

"Who's the witch?" she choked out, hearing the guttural rasp of panic in her voice. The crowd quieted and stilled, one man's arm around Cam's waist. She let blackness slip into her eyes and glanced over at the blue threads that kept wavering nearer, as if trying to catch her. "Call off your pets if you want a fair talk. Otherwise I'm leaving."

"You can't leave," said Cam.

Blades out. One glass, the other stone. A defensive pairing: one to reflect dark magic, the other to defend against physical harm. Eli was not a reckless fighter, and she always won her battles.

A murmur of voices rose up.

"How did those get in here?"

"Get back!"

"She's crazy."

"The barrier failed!"

"The barrier didn't fail," said the woman who had risen to greet her — the café owner, Eli assumed. The woman narrowed her eyes. "No one is permitted to bring something that is not a part of them into this space. We bring only ourselves. Those magic blades must be made from your own bone." She sounded disgusted and a bit sad. "A clumsy way to arm agents, and brutal. But effective." The others looked horrified.

Eli felt a jolt of surprise and then calmed. No wonder the blades always moved in unison with her body, always bent to her will. She had been made of glass and stone, and these knives were her kin. Their presence soothed her.

"I asked you a question," Eli said. "Who. Is. The. Witch."

"I'm the witch," said the woman. "And this is my café. You may call me the Hedge-Witch. I'm not with the Coven, and I'm not here to hurt you. We need your help. Will you listen?"

Eli felt deep in her bones that one of those things was a lie. The only problem was she didn't know which one. But she was in too deep now, and there was no easy path back.

"I want proof of your good intentions," she said.

"You are armed," said the Hedge-Witch. "Take Cam as a hostage. If we break faith, you may kill him."

Eli stared at her for a moment and then sheathed her blades. "Spoken like a true witch," she spat.

"I told you she wouldn't do it," said Cam, glowing.

Footsteps. A clumsy hand on the doorknob. Eli tensed again, but no one else did.

"The final member of our group has arrived," said the owner, smiling. "I wondered if he was going to show up."

"He missed me," said Tav.

The door swung open and a body lurched in.

This time, there could be no mistake. Eli could smell the curdled milk of dying magic. Sweetness turned to rot. Walking death. The body moved strangely, awkwardly, as if new to the world. As a child, Eli had learned to read these signs and understood what they meant.

The final member of the party was a ghost.

Fourteen

"Go into the City of Ghosts and bring me back a sewing needle, a peach pit, and a fleck of dried paint," Circinae had told her.

Eli, a fierce eight-year-old, had been sent to the City of Ghosts before but had never been tasked with a retrieval. She hadn't known it was possible.

(Circinae always seemed to tell her as little as possible, gifting out morsels of information only when Eli needed them.)

"She's testing you," Kite told her, as they lay together in the Children's Lair and watched great white fish flying overhead. One opened its jaws to catch a bird; its teeth glittered like diamonds. Clytemnestra was riding on one and waved merrily at them. They waved back.

"It's easy," said Eli. "I'll come over later and tell you about it."

"It's a trick. You have to impress her."

"I know that!" Eli pressed her elbow into Kite's side. "I just wish she would tell me what she wants."

"She's a witch."

"That's not an answer."

Kite nudged her back. "You humans are so weird."

"I'm *not* human." Eli turned her jet-black eyes to Kite.

"Switch! Switch!" Kite giggled.

Eli switched rapidly between yellow and black eyes until she had a headache. Then she lay back down again and went back to worrying.

How could she show Circinae that she was ready for a real assignment?

"I have an idea!" announced Kite. "I know how you can impress her." She leaned over and whispered in Eli's ear.

A slow earthworm smile wriggled its way across Eli's face.

She returned hours later, knives wet with fruit juice. She gave a kiwi to the Labyrinth, and it happily let her enter the Children's Lair. A few bored young witches were racing feathers up the wall and making them explode when they reached the top.

"Where's Kite?" she asked, tossing a papaya to Clytemnestra.

"Who?" Clytemnestra unhinged her jaw, caught the papaya in her mouth, and swallowed it whole.

Eli frowned. "I just got back from a mission."

"Ooh!" Clytemnestra put her face in Eli's face, eyes sparkling. "Did you kill anyone?"

"Not yet."

"Boring." Clytemnestra went back to watching the other children play.

Eli waited, but Kite didn't come. Some time later, she felt a tug in her bones and knew that she had to go home or risk punishment.

"Show me," demanded Circinae, staring deep into the purplegreen fire. She stuck out a hand.

Eli walked forward and handed Circinae an ordinary sewing needle and the peach pit.

"Well?" Circinae snapped. "The fleck of paint?"

"I can't give it to you." Away from the comfort of Kite's legs and arms tangled in her own, Eli felt less certain about their plan.

"Why not?" Circinae turned finally to look at her wild daughter. The flames cast shadows on the walls that danced to the quick beat of Eli's heart.

Trembling slightly, Eli held out her frost blade. A dark stain marred one side.

Circinae tilted her head and narrowed her eyes. "The human world cannot harm your blades."

"I brought you a fleck of blood, the witches' paint,"

said Eli. She held the knife closer to Circinae so she could inspect it.

Circinae recoiled and pushed Eli's arm away. "Filthy girl! Bringing the blood of another witch into this house!"

"We can *use* it —"

"That stain will never come out! You have no idea what you've done. I should drag you before the Coven and have them feed you to the Heart."

Eli was banished to the forest for a few days, and when she returned, Circinae said nothing about the witch blood, nothing about the magic that would never be compatible with her own. Witch blood is antagonistic to other witch blood.

Had she known that the blood contaminating her daughter was the blood of the Heir? Did she suspect then the freedom Kite had planned for Eli?

Not long after, Eli was sent on her first assassination.

Fifteen

Eli's eyes flooded with black. Her blades began singing, calling for death. She forced her hands still, even as she calculated the distance between herself and the ghost (five metres) and the number of movements she would need to kill it (three). An electrical current hummed through her body. She could feel the Hedge-Witch's gaze.

"You tell me that no one may enter here armed," said Eli evenly. "Yet ghosts can be wielded as a weapon. Explain."

"No," said the Hedge-Witch.

"If you want my help —"

"We will make a trade," announced the Hedge-Witch. "I am not trying to trick you."

Eli snorted.

"A deal, as is our custom," the Hedge-Witch continued. "If you harm one of our members, there will be no deal."

"Does it follow your commands?"

The ghost moved past Eli, not even looking at her. Eli could feel the slime of rotting magic brush her skin as it passed. Fortunately, she was used to these things and barely experienced a gag reflex anymore. She watched its every step. It said nothing, simply joined the group at the other side of the café and quietly took a seat. It cast no shadow. Not even a very strong ghost, then.

"When *he* chooses to. He is one of us, not a thing or a pet."

They think the ghost is a person, Eli realized, the sickening feeling growing in her stomach. She had encountered ghost fanatics before — the ones that swore they had souls or consciousness. Some radical young witches even hypothesized that they were a newly evolved form. These crusaders had never seen a ghost before, never seen the destruction they caused, never felt that painful absence of life, like a wound in the world, whenever one was nearby. A rip in space. A vacuum.

Clearly this witch outcast believed the tales and thought the ghost was her friend or ally. It would have been simpler if they believed the ghost to be a dangerous tool. Eli let her darkness drain from her eyes, and the vision of magical tendrils straining toward the sucking emptiness of the ghost vanished. She turned to the

Hedge-Witch with her palms up, empty. A sign of peace, of tentative trust. The Hedge-Witch nodded.

"What's the trade?" Eli asked, intentionally relaxing her stance.

"All business, isn't she?" someone commented.

"I thought you said she was fun," complained another.

"How did she trick you into giving her your keys?"

Eli kept her eyes locked on the witch's. The witch's pupils shrunk into narrow slits, quivered, and then expanded, mixing with the milky whiteness of her eyes.

"You help us, and we help you," the Hedge-Witch told her.

"That's not enough."

"I can't tell you the assignment until you've joined us. It's … sensitive information. But if you agree to work with us, then we will get you back to the City of Eyes." Her eyes glittered, and the edge of her mouth twitched. "We know you've been trapped here."

Thanks to Cam, she thought, cursing herself for thinking violence was her only currency, when information could be so much more valuable.

She could be lying, but Eli didn't think so. For all the Hedge-Witch's bold talk, she was desperate for her aid, and there was power here, she could feel it. There was also the matter of her unfinished assignment. Circinae's words rang in her head. *Finish what you started.* But Eli needed more information before she decided what to do, and what to tell the Coven. She wouldn't kill another human. This group could help her find the answers she needed.

And if they could get her home? It was worth the risk.

Eli ripped out three strands of hair, spat on them, and offered the dirty handful to the witch.

"It's a deal," she said.

The Hedge-Witch smiled now but only with her teeth, and Eli could see that she had sharpened her canines. Eli's respect for her rose. The witch offered her own hair and saliva, and when their hands met, their joined cells sizzled, shedding white sparks like static electricity.

"It's a deal," the witch agreed.

The atmosphere in the room changed visibly: bodies relaxed, held breaths releasing in a gust of stale air, arms and hands touching each other as the companions nestled closer around the table. Drinks were poured and muffled laughter was heard. Eli could feel the magic tendrils curling back on themselves and resting. The threat had passed.

Eli felt no such relief. She had made an ally of a ghost, offered her services for sale like a common mercenary, and broken so many rules she had lost count. She was either the most ingenious assassin that was ever made or the biggest idiot in the worlds.

"Eli! Over here!" Cam was waving her over.

Well, there was no going back now.

Eli crossed the floor and sat down on the comically small section of bench that Cam had saved for her. No one else spoke to her, but they stared, and there were whispers. Eli could deal with that. She kept her face angled away from Tav.

"See? I told you everything would be fine." Cam poured her a beer. Eli didn't usually drink on the job, but she felt like she'd earned it.

"Right. Perfectly fine. No problems or potential deaths." Eli took a long swig, spilled some down her shirt, and wiped her face with the back of her arm. "Thanks for warning me."

"Sorry." He didn't sound sorry at all. "Protocol. Also, I'm pretty sure I've been hexed into keeping silent. I'm not sure — I've never tried to break the oath."

"The one you took for this group or for the Coven? Or was that just a cover story?"

"The Coven doesn't make humans take oaths," said Cam. "It suggests we could be out of their control. Usually a healthy dose of fear and a few crumbs of magic keep us in line."

"But not you."

"I'm special." He winked.

"Not your average Uber driver."

"Few of us are. Cab drivers, too. Great position for espionage."

"Now why didn't I try that?"

He topped up her drink. "You're too stabby for a permanent stealth position."

"Stabby?"

He made wild stabbing gestures with his free hand. "You know, all those fighting things you do."

"Right. Stabby. That's me." Eli rolled her eyes.

The Hedge-Witch called everyone to attention with a

tiny silver bell. There was the sound of rustling in seats, chairs scraping the floor, pint glasses being set down too hard. When it was relatively quiet, she spoke.

"You all know why we're here. Controls between worlds are tightening. That's why Eli is here — and she isn't the only one who's been denied entry. Fewer witches are crossing between worlds. They're fleeing the Earth, abandoning it for some reason. I've been monitoring. If the portal closes for good, we lose our chance. We can't let that happen. Our mission remains unchanged, and most of you know your jobs and are doing them admirably. The goal for tonight was to introduce everyone to our newest member, Eli — she's jumpy, as you've seen, but that was true of most of us at the beginning. She's been vetted by both Tav and Cam, who vouch for her skill and her integrity, and you've just witnessed her take the sacred oath. She is one of us."

The crowd repeated, in a murmur, "one of us," and glasses were raised and lowered in unison — a *thump* of belonging, a single heartbeat. Eli tried hard not to feel moved by this gesture of inclusion. A thin wire of guilt wrapped around her esophagus. She worked best alone.

"Eli." The Hedge-Witch turned to face her. "We know you were made by a witch to serve the Coven. We know you've been trained by the witches as a spy and a killer. We know you've been sent here to learn about the human world and to report back to your masters. We have reason to believe you've been in a confrontation with a ghost and killed her."

Eli glanced across the table at the ghost. No reaction.

"We also believe that you have a human mother whose DNA was used in your making. If you help us, we may be able to find her."

Eli stiffened. A human parent? Impossible! She wanted to demand more information but held back — that was the payoff, after all. Answers. Knowledge. Power.

Nothing was free.

Knowing that this was an exchange, like everything in her life had been, soothed her. She knew how to bargain. She knew what she was worth.

"We need someone with your skill set and your intel, someone raised in the City of Eyes, someone close to the Coven. I am sending Tav and Cam on an important mission to the other realm, and they need a guide. Eli, you will act as their guide."

"But I can't cross between worlds," Eli interrupted.

"I have my own methods of travel." The Hedge-Witch's voice sounded like sugar and poison. "I can get you across. But once there, they will need you for protection. They will need you to get them into the Coven to complete their task. Can you do this?"

Eli nodded, but inside she was less sure. What would happen if they were caught? She would be unmade for sure, and Cam and Tav would be killed. She swallowed. The spit scraped her throat.

But if they made it, Eli might be able to discover who had ordered her last mission. That was worth the risk. And she couldn't stay trapped in the City of Ghosts, waiting for the Coven to track her down. They didn't tolerate failure. She had to do something.

She glanced nervously at Tav, who was playing with their hair spikes. She told herself they knew what they were getting themselves into. The Hedge-Witch would have prepared them, warned them about deadly magics. Surely, Cam had seen what Eli was capable of and understood what all of this meant. They knew the risks and were ready for the danger.

But deep down, she didn't believe it.

"The rest of you — stay safe and stay alert. The Sun is always open to you if you need shelter. We know that hate groups are becoming bolder and that the human cops are not on our side. But they will not win, and soon we will be strong enough to fight back."

Across the room, Tav's face had hardened. Their pupils glittered like black onyx, and Eli felt a chill deep in her bones. She looked away, uneasy. As the noise around her resumed, bravado and drinks and worry spilling over the tables, Eli realized what was so unnerving about Tav's expression.

It was the look of a person who was ready to fight.

Sixteen

The smell of burnt maple trees bowing before her, cities flattened in an exhale. Whatever was inside her body was coming out, breaking through the bone.

The pain was unbearable, and Eli reached down with bloody claws to tear the badness away.

She was being unmade.

Eli woke on the lumpy pullout sofa in Cam's apartment, her heart fluttering restlessly. She imagined a delicate lace net of moth wings in her chest cavity, faintly glowing redpink with lifeblood. The nightmare lingered. Eli curled in on herself and told her heart to stay. She prayed that the magic would not leave her, ripping through her skin like paper, leaving her a crumpled pile of parts. She touched herself, soothed her body's fierce frantic jerks and shudders. *There, there. I'm here. We're here.*

The first time she had the nightmare, she had woken in her bare room, the floor sticky with the trails of slugs and her own saliva. Even then, she had known not to wake Circinae, not to venture into the guts of the house that let them live there — for now. Eli had looked out the window where a glimmer of bluegreen cut through the opalescent sky. She had sat up. She saw it again — like a scrap of fabric, a flag, waving at Eli from outside the house.

Eli had climbed out the window and followed it. As she came nearer, she saw that it wasn't a flag but a single brilliantly coloured balloon, bobbing gently in place. She felt it had been waiting for her.

Eli reached out a hand to touch it, and the balloon rose a few inches above her head. It started drifting backward, away from Eli, away from the grabbing hands of needy children. It blinked out of sight as if losing colour and shape, only to rematerialize a few feet away, half-hidden behind a giant oak.

A game! Eli followed quickly, tripping over roots and scraping her hands and knees on bark studded with stones and spiky black thorns. The balloon led, and Eli followed. She followed it deep into the heart of the ancient forest, her head dusted with charms and curses the way humans pick up bacteria. The magic was so thick in this part of the forest that she could hardly breathe.

The balloon stopped.

Slowly, cautiously, Eli crept toward it. Her bare feet tiptoed over velvet moss and scalloped rock with edges sharp as a surgeon's scalpel. She reached out a hand. The balloon quivered once but did not move.

Eli's hand brushed the strange round thing. It was surprisingly soft. The balloon popped suddenly, spilling a bluegreen liquid like paint down to the earth that vanished when it touched the ground.

In the sky, however, the blood of the balloon creature hung in place, marking an invisible door in the middle of the woods. Without hesitating, Eli had walked through it and found herself in the Labyrinth for the very first time.

"Coffee?"

Cam's voice interrupted her thoughts. He walked into the living room in an oversized white tee and a pair of grey sweatpants. Gone was the dapper boy with the coiffed hair and the perpetual smirk. He looked like shit, which made her smile.

"I want to shower first."

"Sure. You know where it is."

"Your roommate didn't come back last night."

"Yeah, I know."

Eli waited for Cam to say more, but he didn't.

She ducked into the bathroom and reminded herself to breathe.

We believe you have a human mother whose DNA was used in your making. If you help us, we may be able to find her. The Hedge-Witch's words came back to her. Eli was drowning in half promises and threats and the electric shiver that sparked through her body when confronted by Tav's challenging gaze. She had gone with

Cam looking for answers, but last night had only raised more questions.

The memory of the ghost brought a bitter taste to her mouth, and Eli leaned over the sink and spat it out. Black bile sizzled in the bowl. Eli turned the tap on.

In one night, the Hedge-Witch had managed to ensnare Eli in a dozen different nets: the promise of belonging, the hint of knowledge, a passage between worlds tied to the vulnerable bodies of two humans. It had been a trap, and there was only one way out now: the mission. A chance to lose herself in movement and magic and death. She breathed easy for a moment. The question of her making and parentage would come later — if there *was* a later. If she proved herself to the rebels, if she earned a place here ... but she let the thought dissolve into mist and shadow. Everything hinged on that *if*.

She checked the mirror and walls for cameras or witch-bugs, angry at herself for being so careless the night before. It seemed clean. Made sense: no witch, even an outcast, would trust dangerous magic to a human. Eli had no doubt in her mind that the Hedge-Witch's alliance with the humans was only temporary.

Eli could hear Cam moving around the apartment. He crashed into something and cursed. She guessed he was hungover. She stepped into the steaming shower, and the hot water made her skin turn red. Last night she had been quick and anxious, rinsing off the caked blood and dirt; now, she took her time. She scrubbed at her body ferociously, wincing when she touched the purple and green bruises on her legs — souvenirs from falling out of the sky. She scrubbed until her skin was raw, trying to erase the memory of human blood on her face. Eli breathed in the chemical scent of chlorine, burning out the lingering scent of death. Then she tipped her head back, closed her eyes, and let the water trickle over her forehead and mouth. Her mind conjured up an image of Kite, her long hair flowing across Eli's face like water, silky and damp. Kite had to be alive. She just had to be.

When her body was sore and the steam was starting to make her head spin, Eli stepped out of the shower. She dressed and replaced her pendant. It lay pressed against her sternum, safely hidden under her shirt. A headache blossomed at the base of her skull and she wondered if she had drunk too much last night, too.

Eli pushed open the door and took the few steps between the bathroom and the main area Cam used as a living room and kitchen. "What were you saying about coffee?"

"Christ, yes." He ran his fingers through his hair, somehow managing to make it even messier.

"Great look on you," she said.

"You don't look so hot yourself," he said, nodding to yesterday's outfit, which she had slept in and was now splotched with water. "I see you're sticking with the whole 'fell out of the sky all bloody and dirty' look."

"I could still impale you with your umbrella." Eli couldn't muster the energy to make the threat sound plausible.

"Then who would make you coffee?"

"I'd wait until after."

"Smart move."

Eli found herself exploring the details of Cam's apartment as if planning a heist — flicking through books, feeling for the absence of dust on surfaces, testing the windows for thickness and durability. This familiar routine helped to clear her head, to calm her agitated body. But it was a small space, and the water still hadn't boiled when she was finished, so she shoved the sofa bed back into couch shape and collapsed in the middle. The smell of freshly ground beans filled her mind with promises. One of Eli's human concessions — Circinae frequently despaired of the little addiction. Eli claimed it made her fit in better, but maybe she was more human than she realized. Guilty pleasures.

Her thoughts wandered as she waited, always coming back to the questions she wanted to ask and didn't know how to broach. She waited until he brought over a cup of strong, bitter coffee to finally break the comfortable silence.

"How did you meet Tav?" she asked, surprising them both.

Cam settled down on the sofa beside her. "Oh, the same way everyone meets Tav. At a queer roller derby amateurs' night. Did you know their hair glows under black light?"

Eli took a second to digest this information. "Tav roller skates?"

"Oh god, no, they were terrible. They skated right into me and spilled their drink all over my new shirt. I threw my drink at them, and we decided to be friends."

"Cute."

"We are. We're different in a lot of ways, but hey, queers of colour have to stick together, you know?" He glanced over at Eli. "Maybe you don't know. Anyway, a week later, we were playing *Super Mario Kart* on this couch, and they turned to me and asked if I believed in ghosts. I was going to make fun of them for being superstitious, you know, buying into that occult shit, but when I saw their expression, I knew. I knew they had seen one. I knew they were like me — they'd been touched by magic."

"Humans can't see ghosts."

Cam shrugged. "Tav can. That's why they're the Hedge-Witch's favourite." His tone held no spark of resentment and more than a candlewick of pride. He turned to Eli with a gleam in his eye. "Why so curious about Tav? You didn't say anything to them last night."

"We didn't leave on the best of terms."

"I have a feeling that's you with most people." Cam took a sip and then sighed. "Hello, caffeine. I missed you."

Eli sipped her coffee and thought about a boi on a bike and a girl who smelled like the sea.

"My turn," said Cam, setting the mug down on the coffee table. "Why did you say yes?"

"I have to get back to the City of Eyes." The answer came automatically.

"How do we know you won't leave us the second we cross?"

"That's your problem, not mine. I didn't tell you to trust me."

Cam watched her for a minute. "I don't think you'll leave us," he said quietly.

"Thanks for the vote of confidence." Dread pooled in her belly again, a shadow gnawing at her flesh. How was she going to get them into the Coven without being discovered? She played with the handle of the mug. "Look, Cam, what we're about to do — it's dangerous. Really dangerous. I swore an oath, so I'll take you, but I think it's a mistake."

"Won't be the worst one I've made." He fluffed his hair, but under his carefree demeanor was a current of darkness.

"Yes, it will be."

Cam shook his head, a gleam of sadness in his eyes, but said nothing. Eli replayed his questions in her head. Why *had* she said yes? Because she had no other option. Because she wanted to. Because she didn't know what she wanted.

Childhood fantasies of running away with Kite flooded her body with nostalgia and loss. They had discussed it many times, making elaborate plans, drawing maps, imagining new worlds. Sometimes they decided to flee to the human world. Sometimes they went back to the Labyrinth. Sometimes they trekked into the unknown, fleeing the City of Eyes for distant galaxies. Anywhere, as long as they could be together.

Until. Until Kite stole her name from the human world on her coming-of-age quest and joined the Coven. Until Eli had become the deadly ghost assassin she had been designed to be. Then the dreams and plans stopped. One day, Kite would rule the world. One day, she would be the person Eli was running from, instead of to. The ache in Eli's chest grew.

"Any final questions?" The lightness had returned to Cam's voice, although he kept his eyes on his coffee. "What kind of moustache wax I use? Why I have a Darth Vader night light in the bathroom?"

She turned the mug around in her hands. It had a picture of a walrus on it and read "You Arctickle My Fancy."

"Why do you need to get inside the Coven?"

"I'm sorry." He looked down. "I can't tell you."

"Another hex?"

He shrugged sheepishly. "The Hedge-Witch doesn't trust you."

"Smart woman."

Back to the City of Eyes, to the Coven, to the truth about her creation, and maybe her future. The knives at her waist glittered with anticipation. She shouldn't have been excited, but she was.

"Fuck," she said and finished her coffee. Cam was smiling. He felt it, too. "You may not be able to tell me your goal, but I want to know your plan up front," she said, turning to face him. "Any surprises, and I'm out. I may just be a weapon, but I'm a nearly flawless one, and I know this world. You don't. I want all the details you can give me. And once we're in the City of Eyes, I'm in charge. I'm not following your orders."

"Understood."

"Good." She rose and took Cam's half-finished cup of coffee from him. She could get used to having coffee every morning. To giving orders instead of taking them. The thought made her dizzy with possibility — she was strong and alive and a little out of control. *Focus*, she told herself. "Take a shower. Get dressed. And then we let you make your mistake."

Seventeen

Tav was waiting for them at an all-you-can-eat sushi bar.

"I ordered two of everything," they said.

Cam grabbed the tablet and tapped rapidly on the screen. "You know I only like salmon rolls."

Tav rolled their eyes. "You better eat fast."

"Don't I always?"

The server was already bringing over trays of food. Eli stood, feeling awkward and out of place under the bright lights of the restaurant. She was amazed at how much time humans spent eating. Their organic bodies needed a lot of energy to survive. Eli ate sometimes. But she also suspected parts of her body photosynthesized while other parts just existed.

"Sit," said Tav to Eli. "I promise I won't make you take a blood oath."

"Just a saliva one with a runaway witch."

Tav shrugged. "She makes great espresso."

"Where did you stay last night?" asked Cam between mouthfuls.

"The Hedge-Witch let me crash. She thought it might be a little tense at our place."

"Wait," Eli broke in, glaring at Cam. "*This* is your roommate?"

"Only for the last eight months or so. Great place, right? So much character." Tav smoothed their spikes into place.

Understanding dawned on her. "You don't work for the Coven."

"No." Cam had the decency to pretend to look ashamed.

"The Hedge-Witch sent both of you to recruit me. It was a trap."

"Hey, you could have said no," said Tav. "It's not like we kidnapped you."

"Well, you could have told me the truth last night," she told Cam. "Or this morning."

"I thought you'd be less angry after you ate," he said. "Salmon roll?"

Eli pushed the plate away. "You caught yourself a witch's pet. Congrats. So, what's your plan?"

"Do you have the key?" asked Cam, glancing at Tav.

Tav leaned back, putting their hands behind their head. "Have I ever let you down?"

"Well, there was that time at the poetry reading —"

"That was one time!"

"We were tracking a ghost."

"She had a full leg tattoo, Cam."

"My point exactly. You get too easily distracted by pretty people."

Eli didn't like where this conversation was going. "Then I guess it's a good thing none of us are particularly pretty," she said. "The key to where?"

Cam reached for another salmon roll. "To where? To your world, of course."

"Of course."

Tav leaned forward, elbows on the table. They were wearing the same scuffed leather jacket. It had tassels. On anyone else it would have looked ridiculous. Eli found herself leaning in to catch the sound of their voice.

"The Hedge-Witch doesn't think we're being tracked, so the Coven won't be expecting us. Were you followed?"

"Please." Cam popped a piece of fish into his mouth.

"Did you bring the supplies?"

Cam nodded.

Tav turned to Eli. "Do you have everything you need?"

Eli smiled. She thought of the bone and pearl blades that resonated with the sound of her body. They were glamoured to be invisible, but the weight on her hips and waist was comforting. She felt the affinity between things, the meeting of the animate and the inanimate. She felt power humming through her bloodstream. "*I am* everything I need."

"That's the look," said Tav, "that drew me to her." They spun their keys around their fingers once, a flash of silver, and then gone. It felt like a sign.

Eli's heart was racing in her chest. It was like the first time she had killed a ghost. Back when her understanding of death and heroism was shaped by reading Harlequins and *Sailor Moon* manga the children stole from the human world.

"Can we go now?" Cam's plate was empty.

"Not yet. I have questions for the assassin."

"Is this the interrogation?" Eli raised one eyebrow. "You didn't bring any tools."

"I don't need any. If you want to get back to the witches' world, you'll answer them."

Eli leaned across the table, picked up Tav's plate, brought it to her mouth, and took a bite. After she chewed and swallowed, she smiled at Tav. "Then I hope you ask the right questions, human."

If Tav was disconcerted, they didn't show it. They narrowed their eyes at Eli. "How did you get to be stuck in the human world?"

Eli's spine stiffened. "I failed."

"You let the ghost go?"

Clark Kent glasses with broken lenses. Feathers falling like snow. Sirens. "I couldn't find the mark."

"Have you failed before?"

Eli fixed them with a fierce stare. "I'm an assassin. We don't fail."

"Except you did."

Eli glared at them but said nothing.

"So, you can't go back, not really, until you complete the mission."

Eli hesitated and then nodded. "Until I kill the mark."

"And the mark is a ghost?"

Eli hesitated. "I am a ghost assassin. I was made to kill ghosts." Even to her own ears, the words sounded flimsy.

"You're not telling us something."

"Yes." Eli smiled again. A piece of china was stuck between her teeth.

Tav exhaled loudly. "If you could complete your mission, would you?"

"Yes," Eli answered immediately. That's what she was built for, and the only thing she was good at. She was a hunter, and she needed prey.

"Then I guess we're lucky you failed." Tav stood and pulled on their leather gloves. "And let's hope you don't find your mark before we complete our mission."

While the magic threads that connected the world had always been tightest at the points of power — the Coven and its mirror, City Hall — those threads had begun to unravel. Tav explained this to Eli and Cam as they drove to the designated cut site in a "borrowed" pink jeep.

"The main stitch is being watched too closely. And we already know it rejected you," they were saying. Eli winced at the word *rejected* but said nothing. "But there are other stitches, just as there are other pathways, other streams of magic, other lines of connection between the worlds."

"I think that's part of the coming-of-age ceremony," said Eli, suddenly remembering the images Kite had sent into her mind after returning (speaking of the ceremony was, of course, forbidden). "A witch has to sew a new seam, pulling the worlds tighter together, and to do that they have to come to the human world and steal —" She shut up, suddenly embarrassed, feeling she had said too much.

If for generations the witches had been keeping the worlds tied together, why were they now threatening to pull it apart? What had changed? Her mind raced with possibilities.

"I thought witches couldn't speak of it in your world," said Cam. "The Hedge-Witch said the ceremony was a secret."

"There are ways around it," Eli said.

She remembered that day. She had been waiting on their island, lips turning blue from the cold. Lonely and scared. Worried that Kite couldn't come back to her. When Kite had finally emerged, dripping-wet hair littered with cigarette butts and candy wrappers, Eli remembered thinking that she had never looked so beautiful. Kite had wrapped her arms around Eli and shared those raw thought-feelings across their minds. Eli saw dark, then felt a piercing, a change in the atmosphere, and then there was light, blurs of faces and buildings, a doorway in the sky, like the Vortex but different — it smelled different.

It smelled like Kite. Like crustaceans and saltwater and pearls.

"Anyway," said Tav, "we're going to reopen one of the smaller seams. The Hedge-Witch's. The one she used to get here."

Eli nodded. It made sense. The only risk was that the Coven was monitoring it, but it seemed unlikely — there were too many of these stitches between worlds for the Coven to watch them all. Maybe they would be lucky.

The stitch turned out to be in an innocuous side street overrun by weeds and wildflowers and broken bottles. "When I open it, hold on to me," directed Tav. "I don't want one of us left behind."

"The Vortex doesn't take humans," said Eli. "I don't see how this is going to work."

"How do you know?" asked Cam. "Have you tried bringing humans across before?"

That shut her up. *Because Circinae told me and I never questioned her.* She shook her head. "It's still a risk," Eli muttered.

"We know," said Cam quietly. He hadn't said very much during the drive. Maybe the reality of what they were about to do was hitting him. Eli glanced at her companions and cringed at how woefully unprepared they looked — a boy with a backpack, Tav forcing a cocky pose like a performer on a stage. Had they ever killed anyone? The Hedge-Witch's magic tricks were nothing compared to the full power of the Coven.

And the Coven was nothing compared to the wild magic of the world itself.

"It's less likely to reject us if I'm there," said Eli, softening her harsh words. "Let's all hold on to each other."

Tav sighed. "Here goes nothing." They held out one of the aloe plants the Hedge-Witch cultivated in her café.

For a moment, nothing happened.

"It's supposed to recognize the signature of her essence and reopen," said Tav nervously. "She was sure this would work."

Three bodies shivered under an overcast sky.

Then the plant started growing, sending great tendrils of greenblack racing into the clouds. Tav dropped the pot and it shattered into jagged pieces of clay at their feet. And still the plant kept growing. It grew glittering spines and deadly thorns and delicate shimmering petals. Where it breached the sky, the clouds swirled around it, turning to steel and iron, stone and fire. The air suddenly became very cold. Eli could see her breath hanging in the air.

The dark clouds hardened and froze above them. A tiny crack appeared, like an earthquake was tremoring across worlds. Beside her, Tav and Cam stared in awe at the rip in the sky, at the monstrous plant they had unleashed on the universe.

"Hold on!" Eli grabbed their arms roughly and dragged them into the shadow of the chasm.

Black.

Cold.

Emptiness.

Her hands were empty.

She couldn't see anything.

One slow, painful breath.

A burning in her lungs.

Then hands again, sweaty skin pressed against hers. And light, a blinding grey — but her made-eyes adjusted far faster than human ones. Eli blinked.

The City of Eyes.

But as she looked around, she realized she had no idea where they were.

Eighteen

Eli felt it in her bones. She was home. The cells of her body sang to the music of the magic that pulsed from the core of the world. It felt *right*. Joy mingled with relief at having made her way back.

She looked around. A bronze desert stretched endlessly in all directions. Spiky plants burst from the soil at odd intervals in acidic greens and poisonous purples. The land smelled of decay and loneliness. The air tasted stale, like an attic that had been lost to time. She glanced down and saw what looked like a pink plastic Barbie heel next to her foot. A few paces away lay a tattered mink coat. It was as if someone had upended a trunk of broken things onto the sand and left them half-buried. It was strange, even for the City of Eyes.

She'd never been here before.

Her human companions were regaining their liveliness. "I think I'm gonna puke," gasped Cam. He dropped his bag onto the sand beside him. "Let's not do that again."

"I still have goosebumps." Tav's voice sounded hollow. "It was like being nowhere and everywhere at once."

Eli grabbed their wrist and squeezed. "We're here. We survived. That's something."

"Are you trying to hold my hand?" Tav asked. "Maybe you should come closer and warm me up."

Eli pulled her hand away and flushed. Still, it was good that Tav seemed to be recovering. Eli's fingertips were smoking where they had grazed Tav's skin.

Cam had his hands on his knees and was breathing heavily. He swallowed once. "We made it? We crossed?"

"We crossed," said Eli.

"Where are we?" he asked.

"Why is the magic so … sad?" asked Tav, frowning. They were right — the quiet pulsing magic in the air was dejected and frail.

"Shut up for a second," Eli ordered, closing her eyes. She peeled off a ragged edge of fingernail from her left thumb and threw it onto the ground. Where it landed, she felt the vibrations ripple through sand and soil and bedrock. She waited for the vibrations to come up against the Labyrinth, the invisible passageways she knew so well.

Nothing.

She frowned, ripped another nail off — this time accidentally catching the edge of her skin and leaving a bloody flap — and threw it down harder. It disappeared into the earth and vanished, swallowed by the world. Nothing.

She opened her eyes.

"What?" asked Tav. They looked like they had been holding their breath. "What is it? Are we lost?"

"Yes and no," said Eli slowly, marvelling at what she had discovered. "We're in the wastelands."

"Where are all the glittering palaces and deadly beautiful faeries?" Cam looked up at her.

"You never paid attention to the Hedge-Witch's lessons, did you?" Tav sighed.

"We're not all teacher's pets."

"Did she tell you anything about the wastelands?" asked Eli.

"No," said Tav, frowning. "She told us about the Coven, and the chaotic magic, and a few basic charms and tricks to survive. They were mostly 'how to not get killed' classes. She hadn't originally planned on us coming here, although several of us wanted —"

Cam nudged them and they fell silent. Eli wondered what was left unsaid.

"So you wanted to vacation in the deadly City of Eyes? This trip is going to be a disappointment," said Eli with forced lightness. "We're not used to tourists."

Tav shook their head. "Not to vacation —"

"Tav's always talking big plans." Cam laughed. "They're a dreamer. Some kind of magic-hunting Indiana Jones."

"What I want —"

"What I want is a large iced coffee," said Cam. "And a chocolate muffin. Where's the closest Starbucks?"

"Everyone wants something," said Eli grimly. She could hear the fervour in Tav's voice, and it made her skin itch. What was Cam stopping Tav from telling her? But she didn't have time to analyze the strangeness of humans today. She grabbed Cam's bag and threw it over her shoulder. Then she started walking.

"Where are you going?" Tav called after her. "I thought you said we were lost!"

"It doesn't matter!" Eli called back cheerfully. "No one returns from the wastelands."

Nineteen

A cherry-red sun was overhead, moving through the sky as the City of Ghosts danced wildly around it. The star burned the landscape with its hungry gaze.

Eli could tell that her companions were growing tired: Cam had tried to keep up a running commentary on the sad landscape and the red star but had fallen silent over an hour ago, saving his energy for the panting breaths that punctuated his steps. Tav had said very little.

Once, when the two had fallen behind, Eli could make out anxious whispers in low voices. Cam sounded worried. Words like "hurt" and "reckless" fluttered uneasily in the space between them. Eli wondered what mistake Tav had been about to make — or might still make. The thought thrilled her. Eli let them argue and pretended she heard nothing.

Eli marched them in a straight line for several hours. The spiny plants thickened to a dense greygreen shrub that stabbed and clung to their bodies as if in desperation. A few thin red streams, like a damaged capillary network, trickled above the sand, the water droplets burning when they touched skin. Boulders were strewn haphazardly in the brush. And, of course, there continued to be junk: tarnished silver chains and bottle caps and a mouldy Twister mat. It reminded Eli of the children's hoard of stolen toys, only abandoned and left to rot.

Eli had never seen any of these plants or stones before and was starting to feel strangely sorry for them. She let her hand linger on a beautiful, forgotten rock that had a gold-and-black sheen to it. It wasn't granite, but they were both made of stone, and that had to count for something.

"Stop that." She pulled Cam away from a prickly bush that had released dozens of thin needles into his ankle.

"I'm doing your world a favour," he said, kicking at it again. "Someone needs to weed this place."

Eli hissed. Cam drew back, startled. She pulled him close, their noses almost touching. "These plants are not like the ones you grow on your balcony. Offend them and there will be consequences."

"Okay, okay, I'm sorry." He moved closer to Tav, and the two of them kept a distance from Eli for a time.

What she had said was partly true: if you offended the trees in the forest or the walls of the Labyrinth, you would come to regret it. All things demanded respect in the City of Eyes. But she wasn't sure these sorrowful creatures with so little magic left could do them any harm.

The truth was she felt heartbroken for them. And more than that, she felt kinship — perhaps this is where she would end up if she failed. If she was unmade. Her parts would be tossed to the sand, then left to be forgotten.

She knew instinctively that if there was ever a place and time for gentleness, it was the wastelands. She could almost feel the pain of the land as it gave way to the pressure of footsteps. They were bruising its skin.

"I'm sorry," she whispered to a spiny plant as she stepped over it.

After some time, she could hear Cam struggling to breathe and could smell Tav's sweat through their shirt. They had taken off their jacket and tied it around their waist.

When they reached a cluster of rocks the colour of blackcurrants, Eli stopped.

"Why don't we rest here for a bit," she said, checking her blades for sand damage. "I'm tired."

"Well, by all means, let the lady rest," Cam wheezed.

Tav's lips curled into a small, secretive smile. They nodded.

"Does that mean night is coming?" Cam asked, looking up at the sky, which had turned mauve and grey. "I can't tell what time it is."

Eli shrugged. "We don't really have a day/night cycle here. You get used to it." She leaned against the largest rock and gently touched its surface. It was smooth and cool under her palm. She felt the urge to rest her face against it. She brought her mouth near its surface and whispered, "Thank you." It felt like the respectful thing to do. It's how she would have spoken to one of the trees in the forest.

Her companions were weary and sweaty and painfully out of place. Cam stomped over to where Eli was standing and tried to climb onto the rock, only to jump back when his hand touched it.

"Ouch!" He held out his palm and revealed a dozen tiny cuts, as if he had plunged his hand into a bramble. "Why didn't it hurt you?"

"She's from here," said Tav.

Eli shook her head. "No one is from *here*. And you can't treat this world like yours. Everything has feelings. You have to treat everything like a lover and an enemy." She heard herself repeating Circinae's lessons and bit her tongue before she launched into a full lecture.

Tav was laying their jacket on the ground. "That doesn't make sense."

It made sense to Eli. She shrugged and said, "Everything is dangerous."

"I know that," said Tav coolly. They turned away. "Your world isn't the only dangerous one, you know." Their shadow fell over Eli's face like a door being shut. Eli left them to their thoughts.

The smell of sulphur and dried herbs, a burning feeling in her gums. A tightness in her chest like she was being bound into a shape too small for her soul, a body too constricting. She was a star, a soul, a creature, and she wanted to drink in the entire world.

There was so much blood. It was black and dripped like paint over her body, her mouth. It was everywhere.

Eli cried out in her sleep.

She was dreaming of her making.

Being made was ecstasy and pain.

"Are you okay? What's wrong?" Tav shook her gently awake.

"Nothing," said Eli. "It was just a dream." She clenched her fists until her fingernails dug into her palm and left half-moon bruises on the skin. She was shaking.

Eli did not dream in the City of Eyes. She had been warned by her mother that dreams were dangerous. Dreams could save. Dreams could maim. She had learned to keep herself from dreaming, although once or twice on a mission she had let herself fall into a distressed sleep and had felt the wonder of dreams. She only allowed herself that luxury in the City of Ghosts, where dreams could not harm you.

What had changed? Was it the human blood on her hands, or the closeness of Cam and Tav that brought out her own humanity? She surreptitiously wiped black blood off the back of her hand, hoping Tav couldn't see how worried she was. How close she had come to ruining everything.

At least I didn't dream of my unmaking, she thought and shuddered. Here, it would have torn her apart.

She would have to be more careful.

Tav was staring at her with awe and disbelief. "Eli," they whispered, "you're glowing."

The rock beside her was glowing silverwhite, and under Eli's skin, along her kneecaps, a matching light shone through. As she let go of the stone, the light in her body went out.

"What was that?" Tav was sitting up, and Eli could see them now. It didn't look like they had been sleeping.

"I think it's part of me," said Eli, excitement racing through her limbs. When she was home, she would add it to the list. When she got home. If she got home. If she had a home. The excitement shuddered and died away like a fumbled chord. She looked up. Tav was still staring at her with something like longing.

"This is your world," they said.

Eli leaned back against the black stone and watched the slivers in her own body light up in loving recognition. She shook her head. "Neither world is mine. Shadow assassins move between worlds. We don't belong in any one place."

Tav's earrings glittered in the silverwhite glow. "I know what it's like," they said, "to not belong."

Eli watched the light play across their face, dancing with shadows across their eyebrows and nose and lips.

"Can I?" The light and dark showed the question clearly on their face. Desire. Fear. Hope.

"Sure." Eli swallowed, pulse thrumming.

Tav's fingertip traced the thin silver line on Eli's left knee. The touch was gentle, tentative, unsure. It sent sparks of electricity up and down Eli's body.

"I thought it would feel like magic," Tav confessed. "Like, it would bite me or something."

"If that's what you want, just ask," Eli teased, feeling bold.

Tav laughed. They continued tracing the lines of light as if they were following a map.

Impulsively, Eli caught their hand. A large spark popped loudly and flashed brightly. Tav pulled their hand back.

"Sorry."

"It's okay."

"Okay …"

The awkward quiet settled around on elbows and ankles like a winter frost.

"Sorry about your bike," said Eli suddenly.

"It's cool, we found it." Tav's face was falling deeper into shadow. "Cam still hasn't stopped making fun of me for letting you get the keys."

"You really love it." The question hid itself in her words, but Tav heard it.

They looked at Eli, and all of their earrings caught the light at once. Crescent moons in the night sky. "It's freedom."

Freedom. Leather and gasoline. The wind in her hair. Eli closed her eyes and let herself imagine a freedom that wasn't pieced together with scraps and stolen moments. It had been so long since she had let herself daydream.

"Look." Tav's voice broke her reverie.

Eli opened her eyes. She felt like she was waking up. She followed the elegant line of Tav's arm through the dark and leaned back, looking up into the sky.

The face of the moon glittered silver with gold bruises.

"It's the same moon?"

"It's the same moon."

"I don't know why, but it's kind of comforting." Tav rose and gracefully climbed onto the rock. "I loved stargazing as a kid."

Eli stared at them. The stone, her kin, had wounded Cam and pushed him away, but it welcomed Tav as one of its own. Eli had the overwhelming sense that Tav, too, belonged here.

She hesitated and then joined them. A wave of déjà vu made her light-headed and dizzy, so she lay down on the rock. Tav lay back, too.

The obsidian blade scraped against its sheath. She could feel its ice on her thigh, could tell that it wanted something. She reached down instinctively to draw the blade when Tav's shoulder brushed hers.

Eli couldn't think of anything except their closeness. Her heart thundered in her chest. She turned to look at them — at the gentle curve of their chest rising and falling with each breath, at the glimmer of their eyes catching the light, at the shape of their mouth.

"Who are you?" Eli whispered. A boi who could see ghosts and wasn't afraid of Eli's strangeness, didn't run from the yellow eyes. Who could, with one touch, make Eli's bones sing and her hands tremble.

"I've been waiting for you to ask me that." Tav sounded amused, or maybe exasperated.

Twenty

Tav had been born in the wrong place at the wrong time and had spent their life trying to make it right. It hadn't been easy — cops that follow you like shadows because of your skin colour, teachers and friends refusing to use your pronouns. Shitty part-time jobs and beer bottles smashed over your bike.

To Eli, all humans were the same. Soft, weak, clumsy. Sure, they were different from one another — but not really. When Tav spoke, Eli saw the way humans could turn on one another, could take a difference and craft it into a weapon. They were cruel. They were violent. They were deceitful.

A small part of Eli's mind thought, *They are like witches, hiding behind secrets and walls*. She saw the white men that Tav described, who were threatened by a

Black queer boi, saw the tension in wire-sharp shoulder blades. She heard the threat in the exhaled breath that had curled around Tav's wrists like manacles. Tav spoke about chains, about ancestors and wounds that bled into the soil and became encoded into DNA.

"I told him to go fuck himself, because no one else would ever want to," said Tav, tossing their hair. They were pride and steel, but Eli could smell the hurt and anger behind their words. She wondered if all bodies carried the weight of feelings and memories like this. She thought maybe they did.

Bodies remembered.

As Tav continued speaking, the words pouring out of them like a river full of springtime thaw, Eli wondered what would happen to the men with beer bottles and shiny cars when Tav returned. She had a vision of Tav standing on a frozen river, with feathered wings burning black and red, their eyes dark with power.

She blinked, and the vision was gone.

"The first time I saw a ghost was two years ago," said Tav, coming to the part in the story they wanted to tell. Their voice strengthened, and their wrist bones aligned. Eli could hear them snapping into place with her magic-enhanced senses. "I was standing in a bus shelter downtown, and he looked more lost than anyone I'd ever seen."

Tav went over to the ghost and offered him a quarter, thinking maybe he was homeless. He stared at the shiny coin in their hand for a long time.

"He was looking at his reflection," they explained. "He didn't recognize it."

In the coin, Tav saw through the body of the man and into something else. At the time, they thought it was a soul. Now they knew differently.

"I saw what he really was," they said. "It was sadness and revenge, and I recognized myself in it. And in that moment, he recognized something in me, too."

They stood with the ghost for a long time, waiting for the bus, or maybe for the sun to rise. A couple of teenagers wandered over, stoned and talking shit. Young, scared, and showing off for each other. Here, Tav's voice faltered for a moment.

Maybe the teenagers said something to Tav or maybe they didn't. Eli wondered. Maybe it didn't matter. Maybe it mattered too much. Maybe that laceration was still healing, and Tav didn't want to rip off the scab. Eli was certain that something had been exchanged — looks, words, knuckles.

"The ghost ate them," Tav said calmly. "Not like an animal eating its prey; it was more like … the stuff inside, that I thought was a soul, came out of the body and *drank* them. At the end, they were just dried leaves on the pavement. And the ghost was stronger; I could see its light through the skin, without looking at a reflection. He looked back at me, smiled, and vanished. He wasn't a monster," they added. "Although he did monstrous things."

"He was a monster," said Eli quietly. "You can't forget that. The next one could eat you." But the ghost wasn't the only monster in the story, and Eli understood that Tav saw monstrosity in the humans around them, and they needed Eli to see that, too.

Eli had always known that she was a monster. A monster to hunt monsters. Tav's story explained why Tav hadn't been afraid of her.

"The ghost you met at The Sun — that was him. He started following me around after that, and when I met the Hedge-Witch, he came with me. She said no one had ever recruited a ghost before. I was the first." Pride shimmered in their voice.

After meeting the ghost, Tav started looking for magic, and after months of dead ends and sleepless nights, they found it: the glittering thread leading to The Sun and the Hedge-Witch.

The Hedge-Witch. Tav spoke of her with admiration and love. The one person who believed in Tav, who had offered them not only magic but revolution.

"She understood," Tav told Eli. "She saw what was happening to the city — the threats, the angry young men blaming their problems on us, on queer people, people of colour, immigrants. She could taste the fear and hate. She made The Sun a safe haven for us, a place where we could rise up. Stop being afraid. We could use magic to fight back."

"That's why you moved out," said Eli. "Your parents couldn't understand."

"They tried. They understood how bad it was getting, with the hate marches and rallies." A shadow snagged on their throat, and Eli watched as they turned away from the part of the story they didn't like. Eli felt a surge of fury at the humans who had wanted to deny Tav their humanity.

"They wanted me to keep my head down, stay safe, be careful. And I couldn't explain to them the Hedge-Witch's power — how it could make us strong."

Eli placed a hand on Tav's forearm. A current of electricity thrummed through her fingertips. They didn't shrug it off.

"Every time the Hedge-Witch teaches us a spell or lets us taste magic, it feels like coming home," Tav explained. "Cam doesn't like it. He thinks it's becoming an obsession."

"Is it?"

"Yes."

They both laughed. Eli bravely pressed her shoulder against Tav's, the monster-lover who craved magic like life force, whose passion or maybe obsession had led them to cross worlds. A survivor and warrior in a war that Eli had never seen.

Understanding suddenly crystallized in her mind.

"Cam came here for you," she said.

"Yes." Tav's voice lowered, the undiluted joy now mixing with guilt and worry. "I tried to talk him out of it, but he's stubborn. He worries about me."

A comet streaked across the sky, burning another question into Eli's body. "Are you going back?"

Tav propped themselves up on one elbow and looked down at Eli. Their face was lit up by the moonlight. Eli's breath caught in her chest.

"Yes. I'm not a witch. I don't know what I am, or why I can see magic, but I'm human. And I'm proud of being human, even if humanity sucks sometimes. The human city made me who I am, so it's *mine*, and it's broken, and I'm going to fix it." They spoke passionately, fiercely, and Eli could see a sliver of tooth like a portent.

Again, that image — Tav on a river of black ice, winged like a fallen angel. Stars raged overhead. The ice cracked —

"Eli?"

"What?" The afterimage of fire lingered on the inside of her eyelids.

"What are you thinking?"

Eli tried to bring back the vision of flame and ice, but it was lost.

"You want to fix the city or break it?" she challenged.

"Sometimes they're the same thing."

"I think so, too."

After a moment, Tav lay back down. Together, they stared into the galaxy and somewhere in it a human city that held their past and future.

Twenty-One

"Go into the forest," Circinae said. "Go into the forest and bring me four leaves from the quietest tree."

The night was dark, stars piercing the sky like shrapnel. The forest was silent, watching the girl. Waiting.

One misstep, a single mistake. A root that moved like a snake. A pit opened and Eli fell into the earth.

Dirt in her mouth. In her ears. In her eyes.

She couldn't breathe.

Roots wound themselves around her body.

Where was Tav?

Who's Tav? *Eli wondered, and then she remembered.*

Wake up, *she told herself.* You have to wake up!

The roots wound tighter around her rib cage. She closed her eyes, swallowed dirt, and grasped the dream with both hands.

The dream fell apart like wet tissue, pieces of it peeling away at her touch.

Eli opened her eyes. She was back in the wastelands.

She was partially buried in sand, grit in her ears and eyes and hair. Her lungs were tight. Three crimson suns blazed overhead. Eli wondered what part of the galaxy they were moving through now. She knew they would come back to the City of Ghosts soon, and the silver moon that she had grown up watching from both the human and the witch worlds. They always did. Eli hauled herself up, sand pouring off her body like water. She spat out a mouthful. Her tongue felt raw and sore. The wastelands stretched before her like an ocean. They looked impossible to cross.

Silverblack fear bled into her body, and those feelings could only belong to one person — Tav.

Eli spun around, drawing two blades: stone for defence and pearl for attack. She was ready to fight.

There was nothing. Only Eli and a rock and miles of empty space. With a burst of energy, she understood — her companions had been swallowed by the land.

By her dream.

Eli dropped to her knees and started digging with her blades. Her throat tightened, choking off her breath. Her eyelids twitched like the legs of dead spiders.

How had she let herself dream? What was wrong with her?

Eli's eyes teared and burned under the angry light of the three suns. Her hands became battered and bloodied by rock. The sand under her fingernails bit into the fleshy nail bed and she gritted her teeth in pain.

But she was getting closer.

Don't die, she thought desperately. *Please don't die.*

That would be a mistake she couldn't fix.

Images flashed in her head, memories dredged up by panic and set free by a world that thrived on powerful feelings. Memories sharpened by fear. Waking nightmares.

Looking up through blue waves of light.

Chlorine eating away at their mouth and lungs.

Their eyes start to close.

Eli dug faster, using the handle of a blade to break apart clumps of soil. She could almost taste the chlorine in her mouth, could almost feel its burn. There are many ways to drown, and Tav and Cam were caught between water and sand, dying again and again and again.

Eli's thumbnail caught on a stone and ripped, leaving it bloody and staining the sand red. Smoke spiralled from the wound. She pushed on, shoving her raw arms into the earth.

She caught the scent of pine and vanilla. Suddenly, a new memory crowded her mind.

Hands slamming against the metal door.

The smell of urine and cigarettes and bleach.

"Come out, faggot!"

Cam. The memory was clear and strong, as pain clawed its way to the surface. Scars broke open. The past scratched its way into the present. Not all humans were haunted by magical ghosts, but all humans were haunted.

She was getting closer.

Eli screamed in frustration, dropped her knives, and scrabbled at the earth with ragged nails. Her heart was beating so loudly it felt like thunder was cracking in the sky around her head. Her body was electric, alive, fighting as hard as it could.

A glint of silver.

An earring.

Eli lifted it to her face, fingers trembling. She was so close.

She closed her eyes.

Bring me to them, she commanded the wastelands. She focused her willpower on the sand. She would *make* it obey.

She could hear the angry winds rising at her order, throwing hot dust into her face.

Let them go! She released the full force of her energy at the earth and plunged her arm back into the silt.

She felt hair. She grabbed and pulled, heaving with her whole body. As soon as the shape of a head emerged, Eli used both hands and stood, dragging the body out of the sand. Then she went back and dragged the other body out, too.

They lay side by side like corpses. Eli watched over them and waited. The wind died down. The wastelands were eerily silent.

And then, in unison, they gasped for breath. Tav curled over and began coughing up sand. Cam was still gulping for air, like a fish stranded on the shore.

Eli exhaled deeply and felt the tight coil of her chest start to unwind.

Tav was the first to stand. They managed a few steps before vomiting sand and bile.

Cam was shaking, trying to wipe the filth from his body.

"I remember —"

"Don't think about it," said Eli. "Get up. Move."

"I was trapped inside for hours," he whispered. "No one came to find me. They were just out there, waiting for me."

"I found you." Eli dragged him to his feet. "You're not trapped anymore. Breathe, Cam. Breathe, okay?"

"I was drowning." Tav's eyes were wide. "I drowned."

"Not yet, you haven't." Eli put a hand on Tav's shoulder. "Come on. We have to keep moving."

Guilt pressed at her diaphragm.

She had let herself dream.

Eli forced herself to walk ahead, fists clenched at her sides. She wouldn't sleep again. She couldn't risk making another mistake. She was losing control.

The stain of truth was growing, spreading through every synapse and skin cell.

She was a broken tool.

Twenty-Two

Neither Cam nor Tav spoke again about being buried alive, but Eli caught glimpses of their memories while they slept. Crawl spaces and car crashes, bones ground into dust, a pressure against their skulls so strong that it felt like their eyes would pop out of their head.

Eli watched over them, holding the obsidian blade, ready to kill any nightmare that tried to come out. She didn't know what human dreams could do in the City of Eyes, but she wanted to be ready. A couple of times she woke them, terrified that the sand would re-form in their lungs and they would drown in their sleep.

But their dreams, like their world, were safe. Only Eli was a threat.

After the nightmares, they walked in silence, like sleepwalkers. Eli kept them on course, looked for physical injuries (there were none), and waited.

The heavy shrub was thinning again, turning back into naked desert. Eli had no idea what the change of landscape meant. Even the rocks were crumbling into pebbles, and Eli had seen nothing but a few oxidized buttons for the last hundred steps.

Then she saw it — a patch of land that was smooth and red like an open wound.

"What is that?" asked Tav. Their voice was hoarse, worn raw by sand and screaming.

"I don't know." Eli frowned. She couldn't see or feel any magic in that spot. "It's dead."

"Let's go around it," said Cam. "I prefer the deadly plants you seem familiar with. The devil you know, right?"

Eli shook her head. "We have to keep going."

"Why?" Cam rubbed the back of his hand over his eyes. He looked tired and a little afraid. His moustache wax had worn off, and the 'stache hung limply on his face.

"So there *is* a reason you've been taking us in a straight line," said Tav. "At first I thought it was some superstition thing."

Eli rolled her eyes, then switched to her magic set and rolled those, too, a glint of light on shiny black.

"That's a bit unsettling," Cam told her.

"There's a children's song about the wastelands," said Eli. "The only way to escape is to walk straight in any direction for one hundred thousand steps."

"That doesn't make any sense," said Cam.

"What step are we on?" asked Tav.

"Lost count. But that dead spot is in our path and we're going to walk through it. If we get separated, just keep moving forward. Don't worry." She turned to Cam. "I have my knives if anything attacks us."

"That's not comforting."

Eli shrugged. "I told you this was a bad idea."

"Let's just do it," said Tav.

"Oh, so now you trust the assassin?"

"Hey, you're the one who let her crash on our couch."

"It's a kid's nursery rhyme. They probably sang it skipping *rope*. It shouldn't make a difference if we walk around it or not!"

"You're still thinking like a human." Eli swiftly moved in front of him. "This world isn't logical. If you try to force logic on to it, *it will kill you*. And we didn't sing songs jumping rope," Eli said, her voice dripping with scorn. "We sang it while gutting animals for celebration."

Footsteps interrupted their exchange, and they both turned just in time to see Tav step into the dead patch and disappear.

"Oh my god! It just swallowed them whole!" Cam dropped his bag, eyes bulging. "What do we do?!"

Gritting her teeth and silently cursing the bravery of humans, Eli shouldered the bag before grabbing Cam and forcefully dragging him after Tav.

A sizzle.

The smell of burning hair.

A cold, fishy touch.

Eli shuddered as they passed through the barrier and entered a very large, overflowing junkyard. Old truck tires spilled into a collection of plastic Fisher-Price kiddie cars; costume jewelry cascaded around dead leaves and pieces of charcoal, slate, and limestone.

Tav was nowhere to be seen.

Eli dropped Cam's arm and moved forward, looking around. Shells, scales, and fingernails crunched under her feet. Now that she was inside, the magic was back, pulsing redpurple like a poisoned star.

"Tav!" Cam scrambled forward. Eli clamped a hand on his shoulder.

"Wait, and stay quiet," she instructed. "We don't know who's here and we don't want to piss them off."

"We lost Tav."

"We'll find them. Just keep walking forward. That's what they would do. They're smart — they'll be okay."

Cam nodded. Eli tried to unlock her tense muscles but couldn't quite manage it. She was worried. No children's wisdom said anything about a massive junkyard in the middle of nowhere. The entire wastelands were a junkyard, a dumping ground for the obsolete.

They walked in silence, their path skirting the largest mountains of diamonds and dental floss. Strange tools and gears stuck up like weapons from piles of stained and threadbare cloth. Eli found herself lost in her own thoughts, wondering if the witches knew about this place and how it came to be. Wondering if she could make a life here, with the glowing rock that had chosen not to harm her.

Would it really be so bad to be forgotten?

The noise of metal on rock woke her from her reverie, and she turned to see Cam wrestling with a steel contraption, trying to pry it out of a pile of loose stones. "What are you doing?" She couldn't keep the annoyance out of her voice. She didn't have time to babysit a tourist.

"You have your knives," said Cam. "It's not like my Swiss Army knife will do any good out here."

"I took that out of your bag before we left," Eli informed him. "You try to bring a weapon across worlds and the world might see you as a threat. I didn't want to risk it. And that thing you're holding is not going to be any help against enchantment either."

"You don't know that," said Cam resolutely. "You don't know what it is." With a final yank, he pulled the thing out and fell backward onto the ground.

"Graceful," observed Eli.

"I'm a modern-day King Arthur," said Cam. "Look at this!"

It was a long rod that on first glance appeared to be steel but, on closer inspection, was made from an alloy that Eli wasn't familiar with. It was studded with curved and spiky arms and the occasional toothy gear.

"It looks like something a steampunk cosplayer would make," she said flatly.

"I think it's an enchanted weapon," said Cam.

"More likely a decoration of some kind. It looks like a piece of railing from a dead witch's house."

"It looks sharp," said Cam, tapping a finger against one of the spikes. He winced and pulled his finger away as a single drop of blood was quickly absorbed into the metal. For a moment, the bloodied spot appeared rusted, before fading back to greyblack. "What was that?" Cam leaned closer to inspect the patch that had taken his blood.

"I have no idea," said Eli. "But it has your blood now, so you'd better bring it with us. You don't want someone else to take it."

"Works for me." Using the rod as a walking stick, he hauled himself up to his feet. "Let us go, fair Guinevere."

"Good to see you've got your sense of humour back," said Eli grimly, looking up. "We'll need it." The sky had turned blood red.

Eli smelled death.

Twenty-Three

Eli had been small enough to fit in corners, small enough to be overlooked. In the forest she could pass unseen beneath the great boughs.

The wind had risen, hot and hungry for flesh.

"Trust the trees," Kite had whispered, taking Eli's hand in her own. The roar of the air. The sky red as an open wound. The silver and gold leaves under their feet tainted with the stain of death. A hiss, a sharp intake of breath — Kite was in pain. Kite, the Heir, the witch, unbreakable. Burning.

"This wind has teeth." Kite laughed and tossed her hair.

They had hidden between the roots of a great oak tree, pressing their bodies into the earth. Kite had sung epics and sea shanties as the bloodthirsty winds whipped around their hiding spot, daring the world to take them.

They had been spared, that time.

Only a single red freckle on Kite's back — the only scar she carried — reminded them of how close they had come to disappearing.

How close Eli had come to losing her.

"We have to hide," said Eli frantically. A crimson shadow fell across her body. "Now!"

Cam didn't ask any questions, just looked at her with eyes that were as red as the sky. He clutched the rod and nodded.

They couldn't stray from the path or they would be lost forever, and Tav would die here. *Tav.* The idea of Tav taken by the red wind was too terrible to bear.

Eli ran, stumbling over old tires and skulls. Already she could feel the seductive pull of the wind, whispering in her ear, trailing red dust along her arms in elaborate patterns. Eli brushed the dust off and kept moving. *A hiss of pain. Kite was burning.* Eli blinked. *That was then*, she told herself. *And you both survived.*

Eli spotted a rusted truck and cried out in triumph. She ran faster, pushing her body to its limits. She threw open the front door and climbed in. The dust swirled angrily outside the truck, licking at the window. "You will find easier prey than me," she muttered, remembering Circinae's teaching. Magic always took the easiest death.

Cam. Cam was the easiest death. Taking a deep breath, Eli opened the door again and threw herself back into the storm. Every part of her body screamed in protest, as self-preservation urged her to hide, to wait, to sacrifice the human.

She ignored it. The wind was howling now, a deafening sound but strangely compelling — like a siren's song. Through the dust, she could see Cam. He was still standing, still moving. He still had a chance.

Eli couldn't go back. But she could wait for him. She waved her arms wildly, hoping he could see her. The light glinted off her blades and she hoped that would make her a beacon in the storm. She switched to her magic eyes, and through the red, she could see another glow, some other kind of magic swirling around Cam, protecting him. Guiding him.

When he was within arm's reach, Eli grabbed him and pulled him close. Blood was dripping from his nose.

Kite licked the blood from her face. "The wind will have to fight me for you," she whispered and stroked Eli's hair.

She half led, half dragged him into the truck. He climbed wearily inside, pulling the rod with him. Eli followed.

It was only once they were safely inside that Eli noticed there was no dust on the metal rod. It gleamed silver, as if newly polished. Cam was shivering uncontrollably, and Eli knew if she didn't calm him down, he could go into shock and die.

She gripped his arm and squeezed. "Tell me how you found the Hedge-Witch. Tell me why you're here. Tell me everything."

His eyes found hers. They were red as blood and he smelled of desperation.

"Cam. Tell me. Tell me why you're here." She kept her voice calm and even, her eyes trained on his. Her thumb pressed against his wrist and she felt the moment the panic in his body started to subside.

Twenty-Four

Cam's father was born in Vietnam and his mother was born in Canada. When the white people in his suburb asked, "Where are you from?" Cam liked to say, "A galaxy far, far away." As a kid he had dreamed about other worlds, read every science fiction book in the school library, and worshipped NASA astronauts. But his research didn't bring him to the Coven. A boy did.

A witch boy.

A boy with blueblack hair and silver eyes. He had come to the world to steal a name, but instead he stole Cam. Cam willingly became one of the human spies the Coven used to keep tabs on renegade witches and assassins. He did it for love.

"He didn't glamour or enchant me; I wanted to help," he told Eli as they waited out the storm. He could tell she was suspicious. "How often do you get offered a chance to be a part of something so fantastical?"

"What was he like?"

Cam ran a hand through his hair. "He was ... strange. Quiet. Kept to himself. But magnetic somehow. You knew he had secrets, and if he told one to you, it meant you were special. He made me feel special. He wrote me —"

Cam cut himself off and shook his head.

"Cam?"

"It just sounds so stupid now that he's gone. He wrote me love notes with fireflies at dusk. With falling leaves. He used to get excited about the most ridiculous things — like listening to my heartbeat or cutting my hair. Everything that was human about me was so new to him." He tried an easy smile. It almost worked. "Once he asked if he could shave my moustache off. I said no. I said, 'Love, I will do anything for you — but two things about me will never change: my sexy moustache and my even sexier jazz collection.' He got on board with it. Eventually."

"What happened?" asked Eli.

"I don't know." Cam chewed his lip. "He either joined the Coven or died. I don't know which. One day he left. I never heard from him again." The words shimmered with pain.

Eli imagined Cam watching the fireflies at night, waiting for a sign. Staring up at falling leaves and snowflakes trying to read his name.

Her heart ached for him.

A few months after the boy had left him, the Coven had tasked Cam with investigating a runaway witch who had come to the world for a name and stayed. It was rumoured that she was stealing all kinds of earthly things and sharing none of that knowledge and power with the Coven.

Cam discovered that they were right, but he was won over by the calm healing magic of The Sun, the Hedge-Witch's passionate speeches about peace and harmony, and the other humans who truly *believed*. Cam wanted to be a part of that. Heartbroken and lonely, Cam found family in the group that claimed freedom from the Coven's tyranny.

"They never came after you?"

Cam shrugged. "The Coven doesn't really care about the humans it uses. We die easily. They forget us. It's not like anyone would believe me if I told them about ghosts and witches — and even if they did, so what? The Coven isn't scared of the human world."

"And your parents?"

He shrugged. "They think I'm an Uber driver. Not too happy about it, to be honest. They really thought I was going to be an astronaut." He tapped on the window and laughed, a little wildly. "I never made it to the moon, but this is pretty cool, too, right? A galaxy far, far away ..."

"We're in the same galaxy," said Eli.

Cam laughed. "I'll loan you my DVDs sometime."

Cam fell silent then, turning away from Eli. He traced a few lines in the dirt on the window. Outside, the storm was quieting, and in the new silence, his words seemed to hang in the air. "You think Tav found a place to hide?"

"I'm sure they did," Eli lied.

"How did you fail?" he asked. "I don't understand."

"I don't either." Eli chewed on the inside of her cheek. She wanted to tell someone, and maybe Cam would understand. He had worked for the witches. His heart had been broken by one, just like hers.

"The last ghost I killed …" Eli tapped on the broken steering wheel. "It was supposed to be a ghost. It's always a ghost. But it was a human." When she spoke the next words, the frost blade rang out, and she knew it was the truth. "The Coven sent me to kill a human."

Once she started confessing, she couldn't stop. "I splattered his brains on the bathroom floor and left him lying there in his own blood. He was scared, in the end. I can still see the look in his eye when I took the knife —"

"Stop." Cam's voice had a strangled quality to it. "Please, just stop."

"I'm sorry."

There was a long silence.

"And you think the next mark is also a human?" he asked.

She nodded.

"Why are they killing humans?"

"I don't know."

"Are you going to tell Tav?" he asked softly.

She should have said yes. Tav deserved to know they were travelling with a murderer. But what if they looked at her differently? Eli looked away, staring at her smudged and blurry reflection in the window. Is that what the man with the Clark Kent glasses saw in the end? The lost eyes of a lonely girl desperate to please? Desperate enough to kill without question?

Anger filled her veins and blackened her vision. Cam didn't say anything after that. He left her to her dark thoughts.

The storm raged for hours as they huddled fearfully in a metal shell. Cam's eyes would never get rid of their redness, and the dust patterns on Eli's body would become permanent scars.

But they would live.

Twenty-Five

A few hours after the storm abated, they reached the centre of the junkyard. Eli could tell this was the core from the strands of magic that ran together here and touched, like they were standing at the centre of a spiderweb.

It was also the biggest mountain of needless things she had seen.

"Let me guess," Cam sighed. "We have to climb this monster."

"Or tunnel through," said Eli. "I don't think this thing is coming down anytime soon. It's the junction of lost magic."

"I'll take my chances going up. Not much for small dark spaces," said Cam.

"Sure, fine." Eli had seen his nightmares.

They climbed for a while, stumbling over forgotten and unwanted objects, sweat beading on their necks. There was only one sun now. The star was indigo and its rays danced over their faces. It created the impression that they were moving underwater.

"Look!" Cam pointed with his stick. There was a figure in the distance. With a burst of energy, they ran the last few hundred metres, scrambling, using their hands to pull themselves up.

"Tav!" Eli threw her arms around them and then hurriedly jumped back. Cam hugged them, too.

"I've been here all day!" Tav sat down on an armoire. "What took you so long?"

"We came seconds after you," protested Cam. "We didn't see footprints or anything."

"A time pocket!" Eli's voice rose and broke against her own excitement. "I've heard of these! We used to go looking for them when we were kids."

"In between gutting animals and training to kill people?" Cam poked at the ground with his walking stick.

"Ghosts, not people." Eli glared at him, fear alighting in her stomach. "And yeah, something like that." She and Kite had spent days chasing down the mysterious time gaps that dotted the City of Eyes. "We must have entered a different time than Tav; that explains why we didn't see each other sooner. But everything syncs up here in the centre."

"I'm going to pretend I understood that," said Cam.

"Did you ever find any time pockets when you were little?" asked Tav.

"Just one," said Eli. "It threw us into yesterday and we had to go through the same routine pretending everyone was the same."

"Sounds boring," said Cam.

"No, it was fun. I spent most of the day finishing people's sentences and playing pranks. Looking back, it was really lucky we weren't thrown into the future. That would have been a lot harder to explain. The time gaps between Earth and here aren't usually that dramatic, but time gaps in the witch's world? Those could take you to any time."

"As interesting as this conversation is," said Tav, "shouldn't we try to get out of here?"

Cam collapsed dramatically, flinging his stick to one side. "Are you made of pure muscle?"

"Nice prop." Tav poked it with their foot. Eli thought about the blood it had absorbed and the magical storm it had weathered. She said nothing.

"For once, I agree with Cam. We should rest and then continue." Eli didn't tell them that the magic of the junkyard was pulsing through her entire body and she wasn't sure she could bear ripping herself away from it. She felt strong.

Cam emptied the drawers of an antique armoire and made a nest out of silk shirts. He curled up inside it and fell asleep almost instantly. Eli knew she should sleep, too, but between the magic and Tav, her heart was racing too fast to imagine resting. Tav didn't seem inclined to sleep, either, and instead they climbed over to where Eli was sitting and settled beside her.

"Can't sleep with all this magic around," they explained.

"Me neither," said Eli. "What did you do while you waited for us?"

Tav shrugged. "Mindfulness exercises. My therapist made me do them when I was angry."

"Did they help?"

"No."

They both laughed. Eli told them about the storm but not about her conversation with Cam in the truck.

"I'm glad you found me," Tav admitted. "I didn't love being here on my own."

"Cam missed you, too."

"Just Cam?"

Eli shrugged.

"Thanks for keeping him safe," said Tav.

"Just doing my job."

Eli hesitated for a moment and then took out her obsidian blade. It was the narrowest, like a crescent moon, thin and jagged and slightly curved. It was a cruel blade and it worked on shadows, echoes, and the true bodies of ghosts. "Take this. If you feel something touch you and nothing is there — use it. It wants to be used. It's thirsty."

"Are you sure?" Tav's eyes were wide.

"Yes. Just don't lose it." Eli smiled at them. "I hope we don't get separated again, but just in case, you should be armed."

"Thank you." Tav wrapped their hand around the blade, then hissed in pain and dropped it. A single drop of blood, so dark it was almost black, dripped from their palm.

"It shouldn't hurt corporeals," said Eli frowning, feeling lost and confused. What was Tav?

"I don't know what that means," said Tav, "but maybe you should keep it. Maybe it doesn't want to be given away."

"Maybe …" Eli sheathed the blade.

They fell into a silence that was almost comfortable. Eli thought about nightmares and daydreams and the memory of Tav's fingers gently following the lines of light across her knee.

"Are you sorry you came?" Eli didn't look at Tav when she asked this. It was a stupid question, but Eli needed to know anyway.

Tav turned and looked at Eli for a long moment. "Not for a second."

Eli hid a smile.

"It's beautiful here," said Tav.

"You're magic drunk," accused Eli, who was starting to feel something like that herself. The magic was so thick here she could almost see it with her crocodile eyes.

"So?"

A piece of plastic digging into her thigh. Cam snoring in his sleep.

Tav leaned over. The smell of salt — not sea salt but human body salt. The percussive beat of their heart. Eli could see it twitching on their neck, a delicate rhythm of life. She wanted to touch it. Tav ran one finger along a vein on Eli's forearm. Pathfinding on her body. Mapping a history of touch and want. A few sparks crackled along the line of contact, but this time, neither of them pulled back. Instead, Eli leaned in and pressed her lips against Tav's.

She had been warned about strong emotions.

Everything happened at once.

Cam woke up.

The world caught fire.

Eli's heart stopped.

Through the heat of the flames and the smell of ash, Eli could hear a voice shouting her name.

"Eli?! Eli!"

"… no pulse …"

"Somebody help us!"

"What do we …"

"Eli, stay with me!"

Thick smoke clouded her vision. She could feel it filling her lungs. She tried to breathe. Her eyes fluttered shut. Eli's last thought was of a motorcycle glowing like a celestial body. Eyes were painted on the side, and one of them winked at her.

Twenty-Six

"Welcome back, Eli."

Eli woke to a child's face dangerously close to her own, a mouth splayed open to display white teeth behind pink lips. She felt very heavy, her lungs choking. The ground beneath her was stone, solid and cool. Somehow, they had left the junkyard.

"Clytemnestra ... what ... how ..." Eli tried to find the right words.

Clytemnestra snapped her jaws a few times, barked, and then scampered off Eli's chest. Gasping, Eli realized she could breathe again.

"The question is what are you doing here?" Clytemnestra cocked her head. "And more importantly, what did you bring me?" She clapped her hands together excitedly.

"What happened? Where are my friends? *Where are my knives?*" Her voice rose in panic.

"I didn't know you had friends. I always admired that about you." Clytemnestra's face fell into a pout. "You went away on a trip and didn't bring me a gift? After all I've done for you? You almost died, and *I* saved you."

Eli put a hand to her chest and felt the familiar rhythm of her heartbeat. "The fire —"

"Something about lightning. Playing with fire is dangerous, you know." She waggled her finger at Eli. "That's why I love doing it!"

"My heart stopped."

"Oh, we got it working again with a little magic and blood." Clytemnestra waved her hand. "No need to pay me back now. You can owe me." Clytemnestra's eyes glinted fiercely.

Then she vanished. Eli turned her face upward to the crystalline sky. Breathed in the familiar smell of dead fish. *The Labyrinth.* Her eyes skittered around the room and landed on a single porcelain teacup — white with blue petals.

The same pattern as her pendant.

Clytemnestra, Eli thought, *what are you up to?*

A moment later, a tiny witch with glittering black eyes and a mischievous smirk crawled out of the ground. They smiled, and their teeth were black with dirt.

"The Warlord sent me," they said. "You are cordially invited to a tea party."

Eli sighed and then forced herself to stand. She picked up the teacup and followed.

Clytemnestra was juggling Eli's blades. When Eli entered through an elaborate archway, Clytemnestra dropped them all. Tea spilled everywhere. China shattered. The archway closed.

Cam and Tav were sitting at a table and eating sugar cookies, looking dazed and confused.

"Here are your things," Clytemnestra said proudly. "I even managed to keep the other children from eating these two." She bared her teeth wickedly.

"She's joking," Eli told them.

"Where is my gift?" Clytemnestra floated up in the centre of the room, glowing faintly. "I want my gift!"

"Give her something," Eli said irritably to her companions, reaching for her blades.

"What, our clothes?" Cam asked.

A storm cloud was slowly forming in the centre of the room. "I want my present!"

Eli felt a spark of electricity prick her elbow. "Hurry up before she fries us!"

Lightning struck the ground between Eli's feet. She forced herself to stand still. She didn't think her heart could handle being struck by lightning a second time.

The square pupils in Clytemnestra's eyes wavered and then shrunk. She turned her white eyes to Tav. "A worthy opponent." Her voice deepened, and the sky overhead turned black. This was the voice of an eternal child who had been weaned on blood, who revelled in watching cities burn, and cared only for her own pleasure.

"Here." Tav snatched Cam's walking stick and thrust it into the centre of the storm. "A gift from the junkyard."

"Hey!" Cam protested.

Immediately, the cloud vanished. The sky lightened. Clytemnestra floated back to the floor, full of angelic smiles and dimples. She took the staff from Tav and inspected it very closely, holding it up to her eyes. She sniffed once, licked it, and then yelped.

She looked up at Tav. "A worthy gift. A forgotten sword now remembered."

"It's mine," said Cam.

Her eyes narrowed. "Mine now, little human, unless you want to be the next skeleton we dance with under the pink star."

Cam stepped back.

"You accept the gift?" Eli kept her eyes on the little witch.

"Of course!" She smiled broadly.

"Then say the words."

"You're such a spoilsport, Eli." Clytemnestra tapped the staff twice and chanted, "A gift for you, a gift for me, the children let you walk free ... for now," she added.

"For now," Eli agreed.

Clytemnestra sat cross-legged in front of Eli. "I'm impressed you stayed in a straight line for a hundred thousand steps."

"We didn't."

"Of course you did. The junkyard is the portal. You just needed to open it."

"How did I — ?"

"Oh, you didn't, silly. The magic one did. Don't you remember?"

Electricity in her veins. Lightning from the sky. Everything was burning. And through the smoke — Tav. Tav desperately reaching for something, clutching at the magic strands, pulling them, twisting them, clawing their way out through the matter of the world …

Eli stared at Tav in wonder.

"What?" they bit into a sugar cookie.

Eli didn't have words. "How …"

"I don't know." Crumbs fell to the floor. Clytemnestra immediately began licking them up, giggling wildly. "I thought you were dying, and I panicked. I saw the magic and I just grabbed it. I don't know what I did."

"Could you do it again?"

"I don't know."

Eli held out her teacup to catch a few drops of tea dripping from the tablecloth. "I'd say thank you for saving me, but you did almost kill me first."

No one laughed.

They drank tea and ate cookies and tried to breathe.

Eli could hear a revel going on behind one of the walls. Her body remembered the movements, the feelings, the rush of bodies and hearts and blood. She hadn't been allowed back here for years — the walls barred all adults from entering, unless they had a token of favour from a child. A key. Eli's hand went to the pendant. *Why now?* she wondered. *Why would Clytemnestra invite me back now?*

"She's … just someone. A friend. It doesn't matter. How long was I unconscious?"

"Such a human question," teased Cam, adopting a scholarly tone. "Don't you know time works differently here?"

Eli smiled. "You're tougher than you look, boy."

"No, that's Tav."

"Tav looks tough," Eli said without thinking, watching them fan three aces across the stone floor.

"Thank you." Tav looked up and tried to smile. Eli could see the strain around their eyes, the hollow of sleeplessness.

"Okay, okay, enough flirting. Four kings!" Cam tossed his cards down with a flourish.

Eli wanted to ask Tav if they could stop her from dreaming. She wanted to touch their shoulder, to run her fingers through their hair. Instead she balled her hands into fists and sat up. Tried not to think about Kite's light going out, the vacuum of dark and empty. Tried not to think at all.

"If Kite's a friend, why haven't we met them?" Tav looked back at their cards and Eli wondered if she just imagined the look of worry in their face.

"She's a witch," said Eli simply.

"So is the Hedge-Witch," Tav pointed out.

"Yeah, but she ran away. And the only other witch we've met is Clytemnestra …" Cam shuddered. "I mean, I'm glad she rescued us, but I don't know how safe I feel with witch allies."

"Safer than without," said Tav.

"She also might be dead," Eli told the ceiling. Fingers interlocking over her knees. Tight, tighter, choking the joint. Waiting to feel something. Waiting for a sign.

Nothing.

She breathed.

"Or not," she shrugged. "I think maybe not."

"You think?" Cam shot her a worried look. "Are you still hallucinating?"

"No, just dreaming." Eli laughed, and even to her own ears, it sounded wild.

"Clytemnestra said you needed to rest." Tav played with the edges of their card.

"Where is my jacket?"

"She also said you needed to photosynthesize." Tav bent one of the corners. "I wasn't sure if she was joking or not."

"I never know." Eli suddenly felt exhausted again. She laid her head back down on the cool ground and let her eyes close. Home. She didn't want to leave.

Eli woke in a single moment, sharp as a cut. Her eyelids snapped open. The sky was dark purple, and thick brambles twisted overhead.

Tav was sitting nearby.

"You can't let me sleep," she said, sitting up and checking for her pulse. "It's too dangerous."

"Clytemnestra was watching over you for a while, in case you 'got out of hand,' she said. Eli, you need to sleep."

"I don't trust her. Promise me you won't let me sleep, Tav."

"Eli —"

"Promise me. My dreams could kill us. You have to promise." The panic was rising in her voice — why had she allowed herself to fall asleep? Was she a weak human now, with no self-discipline? "Promise me!"

"Okay. Okay, fine. I promise." Tav glanced over, eyebrows raised. "Okay?"

"Okay. Good." Eli exhaled. "Where's Cam?"

"Still asleep." Tav gestured to the pile of clothes in one corner of the room. "He got tired of losing at rummy."

Eli nodded and began checking her blades for scratches. The silence hung between them like a string of lights.

"You could have died," Tav whispered, their voice so soft that Eli could barely hear them.

"I don't think that was even the closest I've come to death," said Eli.

"You were struck by lightning."

"Good thing I'm hard to kill."

Tav shuffled the deck aimlessly. Then they crawled over to Eli.

"I'm glad you didn't die."

"Me, too."

Another beat of silence, heavy with unsaid words. Eli waited.

"The Heart," Tav said finally. "We've been sent for the Heart of the Coven."

Eli's head snapped up. "That's impossible."

Tav shook their head. "The Hedge-Witch says it's possible, but a human has to carry it across worlds."

"You came to steal the Heart?" she breathed.

"Yes." Tav's eyes were burning with intensity. "We want to steal the magic of this world. Think how we could use it. Think how it could help us!"

"Us, or you?"

Tav's jaw tightened. "You've seen what it's like in our city. You know the way people like me are treated. With magic, we could make a difference. We could change things!"

"It would be chaos."

Tav leaned back against the rock and looked up at the constellations overhead. "Maybe chaos is better than violent order. But it doesn't have to be chaos, Eli — we could build something better."

"We?"

Tav moved closer. They reached over and brushed a strand of hair from Eli's face. They were so close their breath clouded Eli's glasses. "You could come with me. Once we have magic, the real fight begins. I could use your help."

Eli swallowed. She felt trapped by the sparks in Tav's eyes and the heat from their touch. But stealing the Heart, ripping it out of the world and transplanting it into a new one?

What would happen to the City of Eyes?

She wished Kite were here. With her knowledge, she might have the answer. But Tav wasn't thinking about what could go wrong. They didn't want to hear that their plan might fail. They were living on hope — and desperation. Eli understood that feeling. Instead of answering, Eli leaned forward and into danger. She brushed her lips against Tav's. A spark lit up the dark. A sudden intake of breath. Eli hesitated. Then Tav kissed her back, and their hands were in her hair, and they were holding each other, pressing their bodies together.

This time, lightning didn't strike. Instead, it danced around their bodies, as if it wanted to be a part of everything.

Eli had never been so grateful to have a body.

After a while, they both lay back on the cool rock. Eli wanted to ask how Tav was able to tell her their mission when Cam had been cursed into silence. She wanted to know if Cam, too, wanted to steal the witches' magic.

There was something about Tav that was different from the other humans — she could taste it on her tongue. Something that made her blades tremble. And Tav had opened a door in the world. They had used magic.

"Does the Hedge-Witch know you can use magic?" she asked.

"No. At least she never said anything to me."

"Maybe she didn't want you to know."

"I trust her, Eli."

Eli sighed, feeling the tension creeping back into her joints. "I said I would take you to the Coven, and I'm going to. I can't promise anything else."

"I'll take what I can get." Eli could hear Tav's smile through the darkness.

They lay side by side, hearts beating wildly, fingers intertwined.

Should she let Tav take the Heart? Could she stop them?

She pulled her hand away from Tav's. "I need to see Clytemnestra."

"Now?" Irritation gravelled Tav's voice.

"Yeah, now."

"I'll come."

"No! No — you need to stay with Cam."

"Okay …"

"I won't be long."

Eli checked her knives, stood, and retrieved her jacket from across the room. She pressed her hand against one of the walls and it melted away, as if it recognized her touch. She stepped through into another identical room, and for a moment, her breathing stuttered as she gulped air. As a child, she had often enjoyed trapping creatures in a maze in the wall. But before Eli could panic, a wooden door grew out of the wall, vines and twigs stabbing and twisting together to form a perfect gate. The gate opened, and Clytemnestra skipped inside.

"We redecorated," said Clytemnestra, gesturing to the brambles, some of which had sprouted large blue flowers that gave off a sickly sweet smell. Carnivorous. "Do you like it? You have to go now."

Eli nodded. They had stayed too long. She hesitated and then asked the question she had been holding on to. "Do you know what we're doing? Why the humans are here?"

"Why would I care what you're doing?" Clytemnestra was playing with a handful of bones. "Humans are boring."

"These ones aren't."

"No, they're interesting. Bring them back to play."

"Okay. And thank you for helping us. Good hunting." Eli hesitated. "Why did you give me a key?" Her hand went to the pendant that rested against her clavicle, the piece of china that matched Clytemnestra's tea set.

"Oh, the Warlord thought you might be useful." Clytemnestra sounded bored. "And you're so much fun — I've missed you."

"Of course." Eli let her hand drop to her side. She should have known better than to expect straight answers from the little witch.

"Don't you want me to tell your fortune?" Clytemnestra cupped her hands over the bones and rattled them vigorously. The sound echoed through the chamber.

"That only works if you believe."

"And you smell like superstition. You smell like human. Please, it'll be so much fun!"

"Fine," said Eli, then quickly changed her answer to "No. Wait."

"Too late!" Bones scattered across the floor like a constellation.

"There you go — your fortune. Happy hunting." Clytemnestra vanished. The witch child had never intended to do any true fortune-telling. But she liked to break things.

Eli stared down at the mess of animal bones. *This is what I am*, she thought. Then she smiled and went after the other two animals of flesh and bone that had been flung across the City of Eyes, lost between worlds.

The thing about bones — when they break, they cut.

Twenty-Eight

Clytemnestra left them in the Labyrinth. Magic wind rushed about their ankles, playing with their hair, tugging on their sleeves. The walls here were perfectly smooth, as if carved from a giant slab of marble.

The most powerful witches in the world wore dark clothing that burned like an eclipse against white stone and petrified wood. But here in the Labyrinth everyone wore pale clothing and used ground bone powder to conceal themselves from prying eyes. As a child, Eli had thought the Labyrinth was a great playground that only she had discovered. It wasn't until she was older that she learned to see the different shades of slate and pearl that moved like strange shadows through the narrow passageways, learned the rank smell of bodies that overpowered the sweetness of wet calcified walls.

"Come on," said Eli. "This way." She turned a corner and then another.

"So, you know the way out?" Tav asked.

"We can't take the shadow door I'm used to, but they're all over the world. We have to find the one that leads to the Coven."

Once she thought about it, the answer was obvious. How had Clytemnestra evaded the Coven for so long? How did the children grow strong on magic that wasn't theirs? There was no better way to infiltrate the old powerful building than with the overlaid twisting reality that was the Labyrinth. The living walls were their protection. The walls had sworn no allegiance to the Coven. And the magic world lived on chaos, needed it, craved it. There would be no way to control the Labyrinth without killing the world.

The Coven believed in fear and secrecy, the fury of wild magic, and the might of their own claws and teeth. The Coven hadn't counted on the foolishness of teenagers, the power of desire, and the desperation of a girl who had been taught she had nothing to lose.

"We just walk in? That seems too easy," said Cam. "Especially now that we don't have weapons." He was taking the loss of his staff poorly.

"It's not easy," said Eli, playing with her knives.

"Can I have one?" asked Cam. "You have, like, seven. We should arm ourselves."

"No," said Eli, thinking of the way the obsidian blade had bit Tav.

"Why not?"

"Because I've seen you almost chop your finger off with a steak knife, that's why," Tav broke in.

"That only happened twice!"

They rounded another corner, and Eli could hear a quick intake of breath from Tav. Words were written in blood across the far side of the wall.

I MISSED YOU

Eli reached out and grabbed Tav's hand, gave their palm a quick squeeze, and let go. "They're just words," she said.

"Words have power here," said Cam.

"They have power everywhere." Tav swallowed.

"Here they have power only if you believe."

"A little help?" Cam's voice sounded strained. Eli whipped around. He was frozen like a statue, with a giant scaled raven perched on his shoulder.

"Is it real?" asked Eli.

"Does it look real?" said Cam. Eli could see his pulse flickering wildly, like an animal caught in a trap.

"Does it smell like a bird? Illusions don't smell, usually."

"Can you get it off me?" Cam tensed in pain, and Eli could see a trickle of blood run down his arm.

"Calm down," said Eli, drawing the obsidian blade just in case.

"Can't you kill it?" whispered Tav.

"I don't know how to kill it until I know what it is."

Cam whimpered. The beast lowered its beak and pressed the sharp tip against his jugular.

"You have to stop believing in it," said Eli to Cam, crouching down, trying to make eye contact. "It's not real."

"It hurts." A trickle of red from his throat matched the river running down over his shoulder.

"It's killing him!" Tav snapped, eyes flashing. "If you won't do anything, then I will."

"No, wait!"

Tav grabbed the blade from Eli's hand and launched themselves at the bird. The blade entered the skull cleanly, but when they pulled it out, the head rematerialized unscathed.

"It's for incorporeals!" yelled Eli in frustration.

The bird launched itself off Cam, knocking Tav over and trapping them underneath. Cam collapsed on the ground, clutching his bloody throat, face pale.

Eli's nails scrabbled across the leather straps that hung around her waist, unsheathing the blade of truth.

"Show yourself!" she yelled, throwing the knife at the monster.

Frost pierced a wing, and the bird shrieked.

It wasn't an illusion.

"Shit." Eli opened her mouth and screamed as the pain of rotating teeth wracked her jaws. Crocodile teeth overflowed her human mouth, weighing her down, forcing her to the ground. She fell onto all fours and crawled forward.

Mouth wide open, Eli threw herself on top of the bird, placed her jaws around its thick neck, and bit down.

It was rubbery and tasted vile. Feathers caught in her throat and threatened to choke her. Eli kept biting, kept chewing, until finally the bird's head fell from its body, the beak clacking loudly on the ground.

She looked down past the body to Tav's face, their eyes bright with horror and fear and something maybe close to excitement. Eli pushed the creature off Tav. Immediately, Tav jumped up and ran over to where Cam lay prone and trembling.

"You're okay, you're going to be okay." Tav staunched the bleeding with their hands. Eli could tell that they were superficial wounds and that he was suffering from shock rather than blood loss.

She lumbered toward them.

Cam moaned in terror as her shadow fell across his body.

"Stop!" Tav's voice was harsh as they whipped around, eyes falling on Eli. "Don't come any closer."

Eli saw herself reflected in their eyes. A girl on all fours, with crocodile teeth spilling out of her mouth. Eyes like slits in her face.

A monster.

Suddenly, she understood — they were afraid of her.

Her eyes fell to the discarded blade of black glass and then to Tav's hand, which they were cradling against their chest.

The blade had wounded them. Again.

The taste of shame, perfumed and sickly sweet, coated her tongue.

Eli tried to change back, but her magic was sticking, fear and worry and hurt twinging in her joints, slowing the transformation.

How could they look at her like that?

How *dare* they look at her like that?

She had saved them.

The anger that had kept her alive burned through her veins. *Ungrateful. Selfish. Humans.*

Eli growled and showed her teeth.

"Eli, calm down," said Tav, pulling Cam to his feet and shoving him behind them. "We have to find the entrance to the Coven. You have to change back."

Eli took another step forward. She was hungry. Her blades were hungry.

"I know you're hungry," said Tav. "But it's not time. You have to wait."

Eli stopped. Tav had seen Eli's feelings again. Tav was afraid of her, but they weren't running away.

Why was she always hurting the people she cared about?

Kite hurt you first, she thought. *So what if you hurt her back?*

Kite might be gone. The thought of a world without her was unbearable. All those mornings lying tangled in Kite's arms, caressed by strands of seaweed hair. She wouldn't give those up for anything.

"It's okay," said Tav. "It's going to be okay."

Tav was nothing like Kite — they were movement and anger where Kite was stillness and tranquility — but when they spoke, Eli felt that same sense of calm wash over her. *Breathe. Remember to breathe.*

Slowly, painfully, her body re-formed, bones retreating to the size and shape of a human. Only her yellow eyes remained unchanged.

She picked up the fallen blades and sheathed them.

"How deep is it?" she asked, refusing to meet Tav's eyes.

"Shallow. He'll be okay."

"I can speak for myself," said Cam. "And 'okay' is definitely the wrong word." But he managed a shaky smile. "Luckily for you, I'm very tough and manly."

"Very." Tav grinned.

Eli took a breath. "I'm going to look for the magic, to see if I can track it to the Coven." She switched to her pure black eyes. Threads of magic criss-crossed one another in the hallway, strings of pure light that stretched between every single body and object and made-thing. Animate and inanimate, living and dead. The network of power that made up the world.

Eli tried to sort through the kaleidoscope of colours and shapes that was a world made entirely of magic. A wave of nausea swept through her body.

Tangles of hurt and anger buzzed furiously in the air, lighting up strands of light that flowed between Cam, Eli, and Tav. A few threads even connected them to the dead body of the monster that was still lying on the ground, looking like something that belonged in a curiosity shop. It looked fake now, like a giant puppet.

She started coughing up ash and smoke and petals.

"Eli?"

She waved them away. "Too much magic," she gasped. When the coughing fit subsided, she reached out with her hands, searching for the crease of a shadow door or the fold of the Children's Lair. Seeking the invisible doors that connected the Labyrinth to the City of Eyes.

Her hands came away empty. Frustrated, she drew the frost blade to enhance her truth sight. She tried to forget that Tav and Cam were watching her. In the City of Eyes, she was used to being watched — but this felt different. More intimate. Not the cold disinterest of walls or trees or witches. Eli exhaled and tried to clear her head. Hand tightening around the shard of ice, she looked again.

One strand, a glittering gold, was brighter than the rest, clearly visible to her magic sight.

Eli grabbed a hold of it. It was warm and soft and sturdy. She began to pull herself along as it wound through the Labyrinth.

"I guess we should follow her?" Cam's voice seemed to come from a long way away.

"She's tracking the magic. Touching it, holding it in her hand," said Tav. "I never thought to try."

"You can see it?" asked Cam.

"You can't?"

Walls seemed to switch and grow and shrink around the gentle golden glow. They followed the thread through the shifting maze of the Labyrinth. Soon, they came to a place where the thread ended — or rather where it emerged from one place to another. It disappeared down into nothingness. Kneeling down, Eli felt the familiar rough edges of a shadow door, and she was willing to bet anything that it led straight into the Coven. When her fingers brushed the door, it lit up, as if illuminated by a thousand fireflies. She exhaled, and that breath nudged the door open. Through the hole in the ground, there was only darkness, and the smell of power.

This was where she would find answers.

Eli's hand slipped into the cool darkness that lay beyond the door.

"Here," she said, her voice hoarse.

"I see it," said Tav. Guiding Cam, they stepped forward.

The ground opened up and they fell through bedrock, fossil, everything.

Twenty-Nine

When Eli felt a cool hard floor under her feet, she opened her eyes again — one magic black eye, one reptilian yellow.

Her heart sank. "We're not in the Coven."

"It's like the Labyrinth, but not," said Tav, brushing a piece of mica from their hair.

They were right. Eli looked around the dimly lit chamber. Torches burned faintly on the walls. Eli closed her eyes. When her eyelids fell shut, guillotining off the fireworks of pain and purpose that formed the network of bodies and fantasies Eli sometimes called home, something sparked in her body.

The labyrinth underneath the Labyrinth.

I thought it was a myth.

Eli laughed once, a sharp sound that rang out as if

the password had finally been uttered after a thousand wrong attempts.

"Well, we're definitely somewhere. I think we're getting closer."

She opened her eyes again and could make out the gold thread, drawing them deeper into the under-labyrinth.

"Where's Cam?" asked Tav.

"Here." His voice was strangled and heavy with frustration. "I don't think the door wanted me to pass through it."

Peering through the shadows, Eli realized that Cam was not huddled against the wall but firmly embedded inside it. From the shoulders down, he was entirely in the stone.

"How did you do that?" asked Eli. "That's impressive."

"Hey, not all of us are as compatible with magic as you are."

"Well, at least you aren't bleeding anymore." This was the closest Eli could get to an apology.

"I'll take that as your version of 'Oh Cam, I was so worried. I'm glad you're alive.'"

"Oh Cam, I was so worried. I'm glad you're alive," she repeated in a monotone.

"Very funny. Are you going to get me out of here, or what? You can, can't you?" His voice was strained.

"We'll get you out," said Tav, raising an eyebrow at Eli. "Right?"

"I have no idea." Eli stared admiringly at the way stone flowed easily into flesh. "You look good like this."

"I always look good, and I'm ready for you to do your magic-girl thing anytime."

She shook her head. "It doesn't work like that. There aren't rules, just agreements. Sometimes those agreements are based on force — you can make a lion jump through a hoop if you scare and hurt him enough. You can do the same thing here. Other agreements are based on mutual respect, and those tend to be more powerful. But they take longer."

"You want me to make an agreement with the wall?"

"I can't negotiate on your behalf. Look, I'll turn around and give you privacy."

"Umm ... thanks?"

Eli moved away a few steps and crossed her arms. Tav was still staring openly. Eli grabbed their elbow and pulled them to the side. "It's rude to stare at the wall," said Eli. "Let them talk."

"Um ... if you say so."

"Eli?! Eli!"

"What?" She didn't turn around.

"It's not working! Now my neck is covered in stone, too. It's getting harder to breathe."

"That's because you're panicking." Eli knew that saying this wasn't helpful, but she didn't have a lot of experience with people panicking. Unless she was about to kill them. And there was only one way she solved *that* problem.

"It doesn't want to be left behind," said Cam. "What does that mean? And how do I know that?"

"Maybe you can move through the wall beside me?"

"No, that won't work."

A few minutes of wheezing and swearing later, Eli heard a loud thud as Cam stumbled out of the wall.

"You did it! Congrats. I thought I'd have to leave you here and come back with a witch or something," said Eli.

"Kind of." Cam's voice was heavy and strange. "It kind of worked." Eli finally turned around and burst out laughing.

"Oh my god."

"Stop it."

"Oh my *god*."

"It's not funny."

"It's very funny, Cam."

"Okay. It's a little funny." He offered up a half smile.

From Cam's feet to his shoulders, his body was covered in stones. Not a few solid plates like armour, but tiny pebbles and sharp rocks, clumps of splotchy granite and smooth freckled stones. There were flecks of agate on his knuckles and kneecaps. His T-shirt was already shredding.

Tav grinned. "The punk rock look you always wanted."

Cam gave them a dirty look. "It wanted to come with me."

"It must know something we don't," said Eli, electrical currents humming through her arms and legs. "Maybe it wants to help."

"You think?"

"No. I think it just got bored being down here. Looks like no one's been in this spot for ages — doesn't it feel dead to you?"

"I don't know."

"Is that why I can't see the magic anymore?" asked Tav.

"Could be. It's weaker here."

Cam moved closer to Eli, picking at a piece of limestone on his elbow. "So where are we, exactly?"

"Oh, lost again."

"You don't sound too worried."

Somewhere overhead, the sounds of a great monster crying out for vengeance echoed across the Labyrinth and shook the walls of the cavern.

"Better than being found," she said grimly. Blackness pooled in her eyes, blotting out the reptilian irises. Now she could see every glimmer of magic. She found the golden thread. "Let's keep going."

They made their way through the under-labyrinth. The tunnels were dimly lit by patches of phosphorescent moss and a few torches that burned with an eerie constancy, never flickering or fading.

"Hey, at least now you can tell the boys you'll really rock their world," said Tav.

He groaned. "How can I go home like this?"

Eli wondered that, too, but kept her worries to herself.

"Who put these here?" Tav asked, stopping before a steady white flame.

"I'm wondering *why*," replied Eli. "A labyrinth underneath the Labyrinth? I don't think even the children know about this. It was just a legend, a story we told sometimes."

"Maybe they just didn't tell you," Cam said.

The thought disturbed Eli so much that she fell silent, trudging along with her aching feet. She was running on adrenalin and caffeine and wondered how much longer her body would hold out.

The tunnel widened, and a draft whipped around their hair and shoulders. The pebbles on Cam's arms rattled faintly. "Maybe we're getting close to an exit!"

"I don't know. Wind doesn't work logically here, remember?"

Cam shrugged. "Even magic winds can't be trapped underground forever, Eli."

Eli stopped and stared at him. "That's the smartest thing you've ever said."

"Rude!" Cam pretended to be offended, but a small smile slipped out. The stones on Cam's body rubbed against each other as he moved, making a sound like rainfall on a roof.

Their footsteps echoed now, thunderous, like the beginning of an earthquake. With each step, Eli felt they were moving further away from the world she knew and deeper into a world of nightmares and rumours, magical echoes and forgotten powers. She was colder than she had ever been. She felt cold deep in her finger bones and obsidian-speckled veins. She felt cold the way a human feels cold in the winter.

ADAN JERREAT-POOLE

"I'll never take you for granite," Tav was saying, flicking a pebble on Cam's shoulder.

"One more, White, you get one more."

Eli froze. "What did you just say?"

"I said they get one more."

"He can't handle the pun-ishment." Tav winked at Eli.

"Your surname is White?"

"Yes, Eli. Most humans have two names."

Eli stared at the ground, watching her feet moving one after the other. Getting lost in the rhythm.

It was a common last name. It was just a coincidence, nothing more.

Her blades trembled at her hips. She ignored them.

She looked up. Cam was watching her, his eyes clouded with mistrust.

"Hey, now you can start over and have a blank slate — is there slate on you?" Tav was still light and energy, oblivious to the tension that was rising like steam between Cam and Eli.

"I don't know what slate looks like," he said slowly. "I'm not a geologist."

"We'll have to find you one," said Eli, keeping her voice even.

"I feel something!" Tav suddenly grabbed her arm. "We're closer to the source of the magic, aren't we?"

Eli could feel it, too. The gold light was brighter now, the thread of magic strong and clear. They were getting closer.

"I see it, too," said Cam.

The light felt familiar to Eli. Tav was laughing, the kind of laughter that bubbles out of your body like a shaken bottle of champagne. The fear fell from their bodies as they moved toward the light, breath quickening, palms sweaty. The light became blinding, and Eli slowed her pace and shielded her eyes, squinting through the glare.

"Is it another door?" Cam asked.

The light slowly dimmed, and a strong scent washed over their bodies, filling their mouths and ears and making their eyes water and burn —

Salt.

Sea salt.

Pressed into the wall, like a fossil embedded in stone, was Kite.

thirty

That morning, the one Eli could never forget, the easterly squalls had carried the scent of sage and mint into her room. She breathed deeply, filling her lungs with oxygen and hope.

Today she would be free of her mother.

The witches.

The world.

Eli had not slept that night, twitching in her skin. She felt electric, as if all of her nerves were firing at once. She had polished her blades until they gleamed and watched the glow of the moon through her single window.

Eli didn't leave a note for Circinae. It wasn't unusual for her to slip out to meet Kite or frolic with the blood-thirsty children in the Labyrinth. Somehow, Circinae could always find her. The Coven could always find her.

Something about her making, something about her body, about ownership and motherhood and power.

Kite had told Eli those chains could be broken. And by the time Circinae discovered their treachery, it would be too late. They would be free.

Eli slipped out the window and followed the path she knew so well, the steps and feelings and prayers that brought her to Kite. She walked away from the only home she had ever known.

She didn't look back.

115 north, 48 northwest, counter-clockwise, a piece of hair as a sacrificial offering. The glittering icy river appeared. The trees. The island. Kite hadn't arrived yet — Eli was early. She lay down on the rocky edge of their island and let her hand trail in the water. Closed her eyes and remembered Kite's face when she told Eli they were leaving for good. *You can be free, I know it.*

Eli wondered which of the heartstrings she had to cut to be free. Which tendon or bone tethered her to Circinae. She would cut them all out of her and be reborn.

The sky turned rust red and then peeled into grey and white. Eli's fingers pruned in the water and a chill set in. Still, she waited.

It felt like days passed, but she had no way of knowing. Before, Kite had always been waiting for her. Kite was here. Kite could find her. They found each other. A prick of worry stabbed at her fingertips and she wondered if the Witch Lord had taken her. No, surely if that were the case, Circinae would be dragging Eli home for punishment. Eli tried to force her mind to the future and the past — anything but the present.

But the thoughts lingered. The threat of the witches who ruled the world without empathy polluted the sacred space she had carved out of the land with Kite. The river was empty. All the creatures that came to die for Kite, longing to be devoured by her, were gone. The sky seemed thin and strained, like a gauze bandage over a bloody wound.

A whisper in the woods. Eli stood, hands near her blades, and turned around.

A mirage, a glimmer, almost a ghost, but it glowed blue and bubbled a little, sending wet speckles over the earth.

"What are you waiting for?" it whispered and then giggled. "I thought you were running away?"

Eli's nails bit into her palm. "Tell me what you've done with Kite." The tracker, the bone blade, could give her answers. Her fingers slipped over the handle.

The figure cocked its head curiously. "I am her. Part of her, anyway. The strange part with an affection for a wooden daughter. Did you really think the future Witch Lord could leave this world with you? That she could save you?" Another giggle, or maybe a hiccough, and then it popped.

In its place was a single shell, a great spiralled horn.

Eli walked over, heart hammering in her chest, and picked it up with both hands. She tipped it on its side, and a black substance poured out, flowing like blood. Eli tipped her head back and drank. It tasted bitter and felt thick on her tongue. It stuck to her teeth and made her smile dark and feral.

When she had finished drinking, she understood that Kite wasn't coming. That she couldn't come. That she couldn't free Eli.

Kite was the Heir to the Witch Lord and could never leave this world.

Eli made a decision.

It was time to stop playing with children. It was time to stop being a child.

Eli would harden her heart. She would become the weapon she had been made to be. She would take her place between worlds.

Finally, after all these years and promises and plans, she understood.

It was time to grow up.

The body in the wall wasn't Kite as Eli remembered her, all hair and arms and music, flowing and pulsing with life. She had been replaced by a sketch, or a mannequin, a thin outline of what Kite had once been. Distressed skirts and dirty hair. Stillness where there should have been slow, mesmerizing movement. Even her face was frozen in a blank doll-like expression.

"Kite." Eli's breath caught in her throat. She stepped up to her beautiful friend and, fingers trembling, reached out and brushed a strand of silverblue hair from her forehead.

Kite gasped like a drowning sailor.

"Kite!" Eli grabbed her face and pressed her forehead against hers. "Kite, wake up. You're okay, you have to be okay!"

Cam slowly moved forward and pressed a hand against the wall. All the stones covering his body began to tremble, and the wall, too, started to shake. "Please release her," he asked politely but firmly. Kite fell onto Eli like a dead fish, damp and limp. Eli managed to hold her head and neck as the two of them collapsed onto the ground.

Kite's eyes fluttered open.

"Eli?"

"I'm here," said Eli, stroking Kite's hair. "I'm here. It's okay. It's going to be okay."

"Water," croaked Kite. "It's too dry."

Tav fumbled in the bag, rummaging through their supplies.

"She doesn't want that," said Eli.

Carefully, Eli took out the thorn blade. She pricked her wrist until a tiny well of blood formed on the surface. The blade started to grow buds. "Shhh," Eli told it. "Not now."

She smeared the blood across her finger and lovingly fed it to Kite. Kite's pink tongue lapped it up like a kitten.

"More?" asked Eli.

"No." Kite pulled herself up until she was half sitting. Her eyes dimmed. "What are you doing here? You're going to get yourself killed!"

"We just saved you," said Eli.

"You might as well have killed me," said Kite. "I was hiding here for a reason."

"Hiding? You were trapped in the wall!"

"You sound like a human," said Kite, standing and brushing dirt off her long skirts. Already she looked better. "What's this?" She turned to Cam, who uncharacteristically started to stammer.

"Uh … I'm — I'm no one."

"That can't be true," said Kite kindly, moving gracefully beside him. She touched one of the stones on his chest. "You are very interesting." Her eyes glowed like a cat's.

"Don't eat him; he's with me."

"What?" Cam stepped back.

"I don't eat humans," said Kite. "But you really shouldn't trust witches you just met."

"It's hard to keep track of all the advice I've been getting," said Cam.

"Survival is hard," agreed Kite. "Even for those of us born into magic."

"Power," corrected Eli. "You were born into power."

"Eli likes to talk politics," said Kite. She sighed.

"Aren't you going to introduce me?" Tav crossed their arms. "Who's the manic-pixie mermaid?"

Eli chewed on the inside of her cheek and wondered how to answer that simple and incredibly complicated question.

"I think she's Eli's ex," said Cam.

"I figured," said Tav. "The name was familiar."

Kite stared at Tav for a long time without blinking. "You have dangerous companions," she said to Eli. Her tone was both a warning and compliment. Then she sighed. "Well, you've 'rescued' me from my safe place. What now?"

"We're looking for something," said Eli.

"Something?" Kite's mouth turned downward. Her voice dropped. "You still think I'm a spy for the Coven, Eli?"

"We're not children anymore, Kite."

"No, we're not." Kite stepped forward and gently pressed her lips against Eli's. She stepped back. Her laugh was a spring brook. "Well, if I am a spy, once we find your 'something,' we can fight over who gets to keep it. I know you enjoy a good fight."

"Where do we go from here?" asked Cam, looking back and forth between Eli and Kite in confusion. "I thought you were leading us to the Coven."

Eli felt a blush break out over her skin. The thread she had been following wasn't her connection to the Coven. The most powerful flow of magic and feeling was between her and *Kite*. She had led them to Kite.

"Magic seems to be very emotional," commented Tav.

The scent of the sea was overwhelming, and it was making it hard for Eli to concentrate.

"Are you going to tell me what happened?" asked Eli finally. "After … after the Vortex."

Kite's eyes grew glossy and bright. "I've never felt anything like it."

Thirty-One

The Coven had felt the Vortex tremble. It cut across the magic lines of the world like an earthquake, the gears of the two worlds stuttering and halting. There were rumours that a few members of the Coven had felt it was dangerous to cross between worlds so frequently. Some had hoped that all the made-girls would fail. Eli, remembering the floating heads, wondered which ones had hoped she would die. She shivered.

The Coven had sent Kite. It was her first task since coming of age — and though there was some concern about her naive childhood attachment to a thing made out of thorns and glass ("She will cut you," Kite's mother told her many, many times. "It's in the nature of the material.") — the Witch Lord decided it was time for Kite to prove her loyalty.

Eli shifted away from her friend's luminous face. Kite was loyal to the Coven. Not to her.

Before she left the Coven chambers, Kite had been given a blade.

"It was small," she said, "like a pine needle. It smelled like the rain. They told me it had been made when you were made, Eli. And that if it pierced your heart, you would return to your original state."

Eli's breath caught in her chest. "So you were sent to kill me." She tried to make her tone flat and matter-of-fact. Kite reached out a hand and Eli managed not to flinch as a damp finger pressed against her temple. Strangely, it was soothing.

"No, dear," said Kite kindly. "I was sent to repurpose you."

"Eli's not a thing!" Cam jumped in. "She's not an object, not like a —"

"Stone?" Kite let her glance linger over his new skin.

Cam flushed and crossed his arms, frowning. "Weapon," he said, meeting her gaze.

"You made a friend." Kite turned to Eli, wonder in her glassy eyes. "You always surprise me."

"Where is the blade?"

"I'm not done my story yet."

When Kite entered the Vortex, something happened. Her corporeal body was ripped away, torn into shreds and burned. It was very painful.

She was stripped down to her essence, her vulnerable magic self, in a place that had neither magic nor life nor heat nor cold. Naked, she went to the girl frozen in glass, trapped in a prism, suspended like a beautiful, breakable ornament. Kite knew that if she touched Eli and gave some of her essence to her, the magic would tip the scales and bring Eli safely back to the City of Eyes. But, as she neared her best friend, something strange happened. Eli refused to take her hand.

Kite had never felt that kind of rejection before. This hurt, too, but in a different way. She didn't seem to understand the feeling and struggled to explain. "Like when a bird forgets its migration pattern," she said.

In the Vortex, Circinae had touched Kite.

Her touch burned.

Circinae, newly exalted to the third ring of the Coven, had clearly been tipped off to this plan — the birds that built nests where the Coven slept were talkative and sly and always dealing in favours and secrets; at least, that was Kite's theory.

"You can't trust the swallows," she insisted.

"She came for me?" Eli interrupted. "She wasn't sent?"

Kite cocked her head like a curious bird. Eli wondered if she was the swallow. "I don't know why she came."

When Circinae burned Kite's essence, Kite knew that she could die in a way that witches never died. She could taste mortality the way a star remembers the taste of its birth, the lingering violence of creation.

She grabbed Circinae.

They both screamed.

(Eli, trapped, had heard nothing.)

Kite had never fought anyone before. She had never expected to be fighting a witch. She was the Heir, a sacred part of the Coven's future, untouchable. But Circinae had touched her.

Circinae was more experienced with the messiness of violence. Kite was thrown forcibly out of the Vortex and pushed back into her skin. This didn't hurt so much as was incredibly unpleasant.

"Like climbing into a nest that is not empty," she said, hair dancing around her face.

She had been unconscious for years (or so it had felt like). She woke on the island. Crustaceans had nibbled away the dead skin and magic while she slept and combed her hair with their tiny legs.

She also woke to a summons.

She fled.

Not to the Children's Lair but to a place she had been only once, playing hide and seek as a newborn in the Labyrinth. She hid in the walls. She made herself a prisoner, surrendering to the earth in exchange for its protection.

Kite had fallen in and out of consciousness, haunted by visions of succulents and scorching winds and a girl who was like a blade. And then she woke to find that the girl was alive and here — and in more danger than she could possibly know.

Kite leaned forward and pressed her forehead against Eli's. "And here you are," she breathed.

"So are you."

A prick on Eli's chest. A drop of blood welled up and stained her shirt.

Eli looked down. A slender knife, no bigger than a sliver, had slipped between her ribs.

"I'm sorry." A black pearl slipped down Kite's face. "You shouldn't have freed me."

Thirty-Two

Eli was in shock.

She watched as a few beads of redblack bled through the fabric of her shirt. She felt a small sting, like the prick of a needle. She slowly went down on one knee and prepared for her unmaking.

For pain.

Forgetting.

Obliteration.

She dropped her hands to her hips and stroked her blades one last time. *You've been so good*, she told them in her mind. She waited.

Nothing happened.

She was still alive.

Tav's hands fumbling at her shirt — she pushed them away. "No," she said clearly. She could hear the quickening pulse beside her — someone else's — and tried to block it out. *Focus on yourself*, she thought.

"You missed," she said dully, eyes blinking rapidly. Relief settled in like a fog, blurring her vision and thoughts. "I'm still whole." Hand to her chest, wrist, throat, checking for proof of her pulse. Inhale. Exhale. She was still breathing.

"Are you okay? Eli, say something! You can't keep dying on me!"

"At least this time it wouldn't be your fault," said Eli, Tav's face coming back into focus. Their eyes were shiny.

Eli stood, Cam beside her.

"I'm good," Eli breathed, and then louder, "Let me see her." Tav and Cam moved away and let her pass to where Kite had collapsed onto the ground, sobbing. Black pearls and seashells rained over her tattered skirts.

She leaned over, the blade of volcanic glass in her hand. The assassin. Living death. Carefully, deliberately, she reached out and pricked Kite's essence.

Kite shrieked and curled up, her knees pulled into her chest. Eli stepped back and saw that the blade was glowing whiteblue, a drop of witch blood on its tip.

"Trust you to fuck up an assassination," said Eli, placing her hand on her chest. "My heart is *here*."

"I didn't want to do it," said Kite. "My love —"

"Don't call me that." Eli pressed a hand against her shirt. It came away sticky and sugary — sap was leaking from the puncture, mixing with blood that spilled from a torn vein. Something inhuman in her body had been pierced by the dagger. She took a breath and winced.

Kite pushed herself up onto her knees, closer to Eli.

"Get away from me," Eli spat.

"It was a compulsion," said Kite, trembling. She had stopped crying. "You don't understand. You cannot disobey the Coven. I thought if I hid here, you would be safe."

"You *can* fight a compulsion," said Eli angrily. "I would have, for you."

Kite combed her hair with long, spidery fingers and studied Eli like she was a puzzle. "The paper birds never brought me an answer," she said. "I asked them. But even the library is forgetting. I could not fight it. It was not my will, Eli. It was the Witch Lord's."

"You're the Heir!" snapped Eli. "There's no difference."

Kite kept combing, kept staring. "You are right and wrong," she said, and her voice was a song. The melody soothed Eli's tension, relaxed the muscles in her neck and back — and that only made her angrier.

"What do we do with her?" asked Tav, watching Eli warily.

"We bring her with us," said Cam. "Unless you know how to put someone back in a wall?"

"Not so much." Tav looked around the cavern. "Should we tie her up?"

"No," said Eli hoarsely. "She'll behave. Won't you?"

Kite bowed her head, pearls slipping down her face again. "I swear it."

"Just so you know," Tav said to Kite, "I don't trust you."

Eli bit her lip so hard it bled. "I don't trust her, either."

Once they had been children together. Once the Labyrinth had kept them safe, like fledglings in a nest. Once they had played together, turning shadows into gifts.

"It's a wolf!"

"My bunny will eat it!"

"Do a spider, do a spider!"

The young girl looked up at the stars and saw the glittering lights of the City of Ghosts. She knew it was haunted. She knew it was slippery and not to be trusted, dangerous, not like the safety of moss and stone and Kite's head on her stomach. But sometimes she couldn't help loving the human world, and she brought back trinkets for Kite from her other life: a plastic comb studded with fake gems, a baseball, the human children's trick of making animals out of hands and light and shadow.

Kite loved this last one especially.

"It's like magic." She giggled, as their shadow spiders danced across the stone. "I wish it was real." Kite closed her eyes and then breathed.

And everything stuttered.

Eli could see Kite's breath, like cold mist on a winter's morning.

Hanging.

Only it was never cold here.

And then one of the shadow spiders kicked up its legs and skittered away.

"How did you do that?"

"I didn't do anything." Kite turned her head to look at Eli. "You're imagining things."

They continued walking in the subterranean passages, following the wind, seeking a way out of the under-labyrinth. Glowing mushrooms replaced the torches and cast everything in a faint silverwhite light. They were no closer to the Coven, and now they had a rogue Heir to deal with. Eli sighed heavily. Everything had gotten so complicated. She was used to the pleasure of the hunt, the ease of the kill, the smooth motion as the blade dragged the ghost out of its empty host body and destroyed it. She shook her head, waiting for something that made sense to settle. To give her purpose.

"It's very romantic, really. You fell in love with a wall. It's like a fairytale." Tav was back to teasing Cam. They walked in front, followed by Kite. Eli, obsidian and pearl blades in hand, walked at the back. Watching.

"The wall fell in love with *me*," he corrected.

"Just don't break this one's heart, dude. I think it will do worse than key my bike."

"He seemed like a nice guy!"

"He wore camo pants!"

Eli listened to their familiar banter and realized with a pang that she had grown used to it, that she was starting to like background chatter, the clumsy sounds of footsteps and the forced laughter they conjured to keep away fear. And she understood, for a moment, just how brave these humans really were.

"Anything else you want to tell us about the hipster mermaid?" Cam turned his head and called to Eli, as if Kite wasn't right there.

"No."

"We're childhood friends," Kite offered.

"What was Eli like as a child?" he asked.

Kite's hair rippled like a river down her back as she thought. "She was an assassin," she said finally. "She was Eli."

"We grew up together," said Eli. "And now she's trying to kill me."

"I didn't want to kill you," said Kite.

They walked for a few minutes in a thick, scratchy silence.

"Well," said Tav finally, "I can see where your trust issues come from."

"It was a compulsion." Kite sighed, the sound of a zephyr caressing the shore.

Eli opened her mouth to argue but stopped. The path before them was blocked by a giant creature with eight spindly legs and eight glittering eyes.

The shadow spider had grown.

"Baby!" cried Kite.

"Holy fuck," said Cam.

The shadow stretched down either side of the passageway. The rocks vibrated in terror, shaking and chattering. Cam's body took up the cry, rocks clicking and clattering together. Cam closed his eyes and stepped forward.

"What the hell are you doing?" Eli glared at him.

"It can't hurt me." He swallowed. "I think."

A spiky leg reached for them and fell across Cam's body. The shadow touched, tickled, shifted across his stony chest. His breathing quickened.

Kite was frowning. "Baby?" She stepped back, unsure now. The creature's eyes moved to her, the light burning like little flames. "Baby's just playing," Kite whispered to them, eyes fixed on the shadow spider. "She doesn't understand."

Eli didn't either. She tried to feel for the threads, to pull them into another part of the world, to open a door to the Coven, but her hands were shaking and she couldn't concentrate. The creature lunged for Kite, who watched it sadly and made no effort to move. Cam threw himself in front of her and the shadow skipped harmlessly across rock.

Then it turned around and jumped again.

This time Eli was ready. She drew the obsidian blade and stabbed at the cluster of eyes.

"No!" screamed Kite.

The spider fell back, one eye closing, darkness replacing the light.

"Please stop!"

Eli stepped forward, blade raised.

"Please. She's not a monster."

"She looks like one," said Cam.

"So do you," murmured Eli. Kite was sobbing uncontrollably now, spilling shells and sea glass over her skirts as the spider hesitated, then turned back, preparing for another assault.

Eli grabbed Tav's elbow. "Can you open a door?"

"What?"

"A door, can you open a door? I can feel them if they already exist, but I can't make them. You made one before — you can make one again. I know you can! You saw the magic, and you used it or changed it or something. You can take us somewhere else. Please."

"Can't you just kill it?"

The spider was preparing to lunge.

"Please, Tav. I don't want to."

"It's going to kill us!"

"Not everything that's dangerous deserves to die!" Eli didn't know where the words came from, but she remembered being there when the creature was born, and she couldn't block out Kite's wails, and she was coming to understand her own monstrosity and the different kinds of monstrosity that made humans and witches kill.

"It's not just a thing," she said urgently.

The spider was coming for them again, and a sticky web was gathering behind its body. Eli kept her eyes fixed on Tav. "Please."

The spider leaped from the wall and materialized into a thing of smoke and darkness, beautiful and terrifying, like the children or the junkyard or Eli's own strange and wonderful body.

Eli raised her arm, the shadow's blood already wet on her blade. She didn't want to do this. She didn't want this.

The creature and the knife.

Kite's cries piercing the silence.

The spider and the walls vanished. Eli's blade fell through empty space.

Tav had done it. They had opened a door.

Thirty-Three

Eli threw her arms around Tav, tears coming to her eyes. "Thank you."

"Uh — you're welcome." Tav sounded stunned and awkwardly patted Eli on the back. Flushing, Eli drew back.

Kite flowed forward, her hair a halo of bluegreen light. She looked like an angel. She plucked out a long strand of damp, silken hair and offered it to Tav. "Thank you," she said gravely.

"It's an offering," explained Eli. "Take it."

"Uh — okay." Tav wound it around their wrist.

Eli looked around. Purple smoke twined its way through the spindly branches of dead trees. The land was dark and wet, swallowing the sounds of their footsteps. "Where did you bring us?"

Tav shrugged. "I don't know. It was like last time — I just grabbed for the threads and twisted, somehow. I think I pulled the memory from you, like I did with the Children's Lair. It's a place you have a strong emotional connection with. Right?"

Eli frowned. The tree branches were familiar, but she wasn't sure. "I've been here before. But it's different."

Kite pressed a cold fingertip against Eli's arm and began tracing the scars from the red wind. "They used your memory as the door, Eli. They brought us to the island."

"*Our* island?"

Kite nodded.

A river wound its way through the reeds that stood upright like an army of bones. The water was black but clear, and the bottom was silty and red. They stood in the centre of the river, on an islet arched like a wave.

Suddenly, Eli understood. She felt it. "I recognize it. But it's changed."

"You've never brought anyone here but me," said Kite, her voice a lullaby. "It doesn't quite trust them."

The balloon creature spilling bluegreen blood. All those nights, looking up at the stars, Kite's hair spread across Eli's chest. The echoes of her name still hung piteously in the white branches, begging her to turn around. But she had walked away, and nothing could change that.

"Maybe it doesn't trust *you* anymore," said Eli, bending down to touch the water, letting the red sand dance through her fingers.

"Maybe you don't know what to trust."

Eli turned to her companions. "Everyone okay?"

Tav was bleeding heavily from a cut on their arm. Cam bandaged it as Eli watched.

For the first time, she understood how easily they could die.

When he finished, Cam sat down, scraping rock on rock, and sighed. "So we're free from the under-labyrinth, but we're no closer to the Coven."

"I'm sorry," said Tav, lowering their head. "I opened the wrong door. I don't know how we'll get to the Coven now."

"Maybe it's time to turn back," said Eli, turning to stare into the dark waters. Something in her had broken when Kite plunged the needle into her chest. Something that had started to crack when she kissed Tav, a fracture that had widened with each step, with every smile. The witch's world was full of malice and hate. It could force a loved one's hand against you. It could take everyone and everything you loved away from you.

She had so much more to lose than her life.

She was tired of having her heart broken.

"What?" Cam's head snapped up. "After all of this?"

Tav ran a hand through their tangled purple hair. "You're joking."

Kite watched Eli with luminescent eyes but said nothing.

"Look, if we go into the Coven, at least one of us isn't going to make it out alive. I've known that from the beginning." And now she understood how painful it would be to lose them. How much it hurt to care about someone. She was better off on her own. She always had been. It was better this way.

"You're not the self-sacrificing type." Tav leaned back and folded their arms.

Eli met their gaze. "No, I'm not."

"You never thought we could do it."

It wasn't a question. Eli let the truth hang around their shoulders like fog for a few moments. She stood. "We tried. We failed. Maybe it's time you gave up your childhood fantasies of playing at being a knight and go back to your normal lives."

"Sure you're talking about us?" asked Tav quietly.

"What's normal?" Cam's foot scratched the dirt. "You want us to act like ghosts and witches aren't real? To go home and pretend this never happened?"

"You belong somewhere, and you have people who care about you. Maybe you shouldn't be gambling that." Eli felt a surge of anger tremor through her body.

Tav's eyes burned with a fierce light. "I'm not going back without it. I promised the Hedge-Witch."

"You can't do this without me."

"Maybe I can."

A veil of leaves fell from the skeleton trees, spilling over Eli's body as she stared down Tav.

Dark eyes speckled with gold stared into yellow irises with black slits. Neither quite human. Eli broke eye contact first. She turned and walked away to the other side of the small island, staring off into the forest, looking for signs of movement, tasting the air for traces of magic. Keeping watch. Keeping them safe.

"She's afraid for you," said Kite dreamily. "She doesn't want you to die."

An awkward silence followed this pronouncement.

"I don't want to die either," said Tav.

"We'll try our best not to." Cam forced a smile.

Kite shrugged. "Humans die."

"So do witches," said Tav.

"So do witches," agreed Kite.

More leaves rained down on their shivering bodies. The darkness seemed to wrap itself around them, drawing out nightmares from the secrets of their skulls and into the shadows of the world.

Cam broke the silence. "Remember when the Hedge-Witch's plants played keep-away with your bike keys?" The shadows seemed to recede at the warmth of his tenor.

"That's what you get for giving caffeine to magical plants." Tav rolled their eyes. "I told her it was a bad idea."

"You were so mad."

"I had places to be!"

"Oh please. You spend more time polishing that thing than riding it."

"Says the man terrified of motorcycles."

"It's just you and the road with nothing in between! It's basically a death trap."

The warmth faded as the threads of familiar stories were worn thin. In the quiet that followed, the song of the stars rang clear through the universe and pierced the shroud of mist and fear. Kite joined in, emitting strange high-pitched notes at odd intervals.

"She'll change her mind," said Cam. "We're in this together."

"We're so close. I'm sure I can find the door. I'm not going back without it."

The stones on Cam's body joined the harmony. "We've gotten this far," he said. "We're not giving up now."

The music reached up into the universe, carrying with it the memory of sneakers on gravel and midnight trombone, music born from the dreams of boys with pomegranate hearts, who were as strong as they were fragile.

To Eli, sitting alone on the last broken piece of her childhood, it sounded like a funerary hymn.

She couldn't sleep. She knew she would dream of her unmaking and would never wake. Her body parts would be scattered across the wastelands, her magic feeding the junkyard. She was so tired — the insomnia played with the wires of her nerves. Day and night had no meaning in the City of Eyes. And without sleep, Eli's sense of human time was starting to fall away from her. She was losing her grip on reality. Everything was a dream. Dreams were real. Eli's body was heavy with exhaustion.

Her blades were hungry. It had been a long time since they had been fed. She had denied them the shadow spider, and they were starving. They were made to devour the dead. She was hungry, too. She had been made to kill, and she felt that need rising in her blood. Her true nature.

She found herself drawn to Tav's prone body. Her blades started dancing, trembling with anticipation. The thorn blade sprouted new growth and reached toward the sleeping boi. Eli placed a hand on it, trying to soothe the knife.

Eli stared at Tav for a long moment.

A human who could use magic. A human that even Kite was a little afraid of. A human taken under the wing of the Hedge-Witch, treated like family.

A full human, or a part witch?

She could hear Cam's voice in her head. *The Coven isn't scared of the human world.* But what if humans could see magic? What if they could use it? What if they could open doors between worlds?

Wouldn't they be a threat?

Eli was a tool of the Coven. She eliminated threats.

Her head spun. She let her fingertips brush against the frost blade, and it cooled under her touch. It knew the truth. The mark had not been a mistake.

Eli remembered the way her blades responded to Tav's presence, the way they moaned and rattled and burned. They had known. All along, her weapons had known Tav was the mark, and Eli had ignored them. She hadn't wanted to know.

She should send Tav back to Earth. They would never make it out of the Coven alive. The Witch Lord would destroy them.

You should kill them, another part of her brain said. *You haven't strayed too far from the path. It's not too late.*

Finish what you started, daughter.

Eli's hand clenched and unclenched around the dagger as she warred with herself, caught between bloodlust and love, between past and future. *Honour. Glory. Value.*

"I'm not just a weapon anymore," she whispered and took a step back.

"Get away from them!" Cam's frantic voice whipped through the stillness, sending leaves swirling around her feet.

Tav woke up.

And then Cam was in front of her, using himself as a shield. Eli felt jealousy simmer in her arteries.

"I trusted you!" he yelled, eyes wild and stained red from the killing wind.

"Cam, I'm not —"

"What —"

"Tav, go! She's trying to kill you. *You're the mark.*"

Everything stopped. Leaves hung in mid-flight. The wind died. Tav rose slowly and turned to Eli.

"Is it true?" Their eyes fell on the thorn blade in her hand and widened.

"You said you never fail," said Cam. "But if you want them, you'll have to go through me."

Tav's eyes hardened, hiding the hurt. Eli could feel the magic bursting around them, caught up in a tangle of strong and difficult emotions.

"I —" The words caught in her throat. Shame settled like silt in her marrow. She had thought about it. She had wanted to, for a moment. Eli lowered her hand. "I'm sorry."

She fled.

She knew that no one would come after her.

Thirty-Four

Too many thoughts and feelings were flowing through her body, currents of electricity that sparked with hope and pain.

Eli needed answers.

She needed to know.

Not why she had been sent to kill Tav. She understood that now, and it darkened her past with lies and empty promises.

Not what the worlds would look like if they stole the Heart and changed the course of history. Not what life could be for her in the City of Ghosts. Those futures that she could map out in the constellations of Tav's eyes excited and terrified her — but she wouldn't have any future until she knew who she was.

What she was.

One thing she knew for sure: she could never go back to being a tool of the Coven. At least, not as an ardent believer. She no longer thought of herself as just a weapon. She could no longer take pride in her work. She no longer trusted that fate had made a home for her. Eli had been changed by visions of blood-splattered tiles and the even more disturbing memories of Cam's honey-gold laughter and the way Tav made leaves unfurl in her rib cage, reaching upward for the sun.

She needed to know why and how she had been made, and only one person had the answer.

"You were always in such a hurry," Kite sighed, appearing before her. Even her gentlest breath was a song. "Everything has to happen *now*."

"We can't all wait forever, Witch Lord."

"Are you coming back?"

"I can't."

"You really care about them," Kite marvelled.

Out of habit, Eli ran her fingers over the blades, checking that they were secure.

"Don't drown them."

Kite tilted her head forward, and her hair cascaded like a waterfall over her face, the edges twitching and tangling.

"You're upset," said Eli.

The hair curled more violently, writhing and twisting over her face.

"Good hunting, Eli."

"Wish me luck." Eli's mouth curved into an ironic smile.

"You are an angel of death." Kite's skirts rustled in the breeze. "You are made for the unlucky."

"Close enough." She waited for Kite to disappear, slowly fading out of existence. She hoped that Kite would go back to Tav and Cam, would show them a way out of this nightmare.

And if not — Tav had magic. Cam was part of a wall. They didn't need her anymore. They would be fine on their own. Eli forced herself to keep moving, one step after the other, moving toward the place she had left behind.

The charcoal door was studded with candles, wax dripping onto the ground, small flames flickering wildly as if trying to extinguish themselves.

Eli reached a hand to one of the flames and felt the skin of her palm burn before the light went out. A curl of smoke, like the beginning of a letter, scrawled itself across the air. Gritting her teeth at the sting of the burn, Eli knocked four times on the charcoal door. She wondered if the house would let her back in.

To her surprise, the door crumbled, candles sputtering, creating pools in the dirt. She stepped over the remains and into the house.

Circinae was waiting for her. Eli paused at the threshold.

"You're late."

Long polished nails tapped against the arm of her chair.

"I had things to do," said Eli.

Fingertips clenched the upholstery, silver and black veins like tattoos marking the back of Circinae's hand.

"And did you do them?"

"Not yet."

"Come in then."

Eli walked into the house.

The door formed behind her like a tomb sealing shut.

"I want you to answer my questions."

"You are not allowed to ask questions."

Eli drew the thorn blade, knelt, and tenderly pressed the tip to the floor of the house. Rose bushes broke through the stone floor, thorns and flowers bursting into life, creating a barrier between Circinae and the door.

Circinae sighed deeply. "I thought so. Go ahead."

Eli rose and traded the thorn dagger for frost.

"I want to know why you made me. I want to know what I'm made from. I want to know if I have another mother — a human one. What am I, Circinae?" The questions she had been forbidden to ask spilled out of her mouth and filled the room.

The conductor who had led the orchestra of Eli's life twisted her neck to look at her daughter. When she spoke, Circinae's voice was slow and heavy with resignation. "I used human bone to craft you, stolen from a cemetery outside the City of Ghosts. I used spiderweb to weave your bones together. I infused your skeleton with granite and hawthorn and glass, with obsidian and pearl and roses. I used beetle shells to craft your eyes, dipped in my own blood so that you could never hide from me. I used my magic to give you a human shape, to make you bleed red, to give your lungs breath. You were never born, and you have no other mother."

The blade sang a single clear note. Eli knew — had always known — the truth. The Hedge-Witch had lied. Of course she had. She had needed Eli's help and knew exactly how to capture her interest.

Eli had no other mother, no place to run to.

Only Circinae.

"I've killed a human. Does that bother you?"

"I've never cared who you kill. I only care about getting power."

Eli let the truth flutter between them like a curtain for a few moments before speaking again. "All those years I spent begging for answers. Wanting my recipe. Wanting to know what I was made of. Making notes, listening, learning, wondering each time I fell if something in my body would break. Wondering each time I touched an object if I was touching kin. The not knowing hurt me, Circinae. You know that. You know what I wanted. Why did you keep it from me?"

"The secrets of making daughters are mine, girl." A smile like a scythe. "And your desperation for knowledge tied you to me as surely as our shared blood."

Eli's fingers twitched for the obsidian blade, the witch killer. "Then why are you telling me now?"

Nails clacking together. A stray thread pulled from the armchair.

"I want to show you something." Circinae threw a sugar cube into her mouth and sucked it noisily. Eli reached out a hand and, after a second, Circinae gave her a cube, too.

"I'll come."

"Your last act as an obedient daughter." Circinae laughed bitterly.

A staircase wrenched itself up out of the flooring, scattering fragments of stone and many, many crumbs. Twirling their way upward, the stairs stilled into a narrow winding staircase stabbing through the roof and stretching forever *up*.

"Ladies first," said Eli, gesturing with the frost blade.

Circinae laughed again.

They climbed.

Minutes grew into hours, which collapsed into days, and then the human circadian rhythm Eli had adapted to fell away, and she became just another magic thing in a magic world of things that existed, or didn't, and lived, or didn't, and died, or didn't. Clouds formed into swans and watercolour paintings and then tore themselves apart. Rain and thunderstorms danced around their bodies, and then the Earth's sun came out and lit up the world.

When they reached the top of the staircase, they were surrounded by an inky purple sky.

"Where are we?"

"A beautiful night for stargazing," said Circinae.

The top stair was a simple platform suspended in the sky. Beneath them, the stairs vanished, and they were just two people standing in the air.

Eli couldn't even see the City of Eyes anymore, although she knew it was somewhere far, far below her. Before her, in the dark galaxy, a blue-and-white orb glittering with lights and life.

"Look at the City of Ghosts," said Circinae quietly, "and tell me what you see."

Eli did. She stared for a long moment at the human world, her half-adopted home, her birthright, her atonement for stubbornly existing.

And then she gasped.

The Earth was dying.

Thirty-Five

There were hundreds — no, thousands of cracks in the world, and from each chasm a pulsing, glittering black light was flowing from the Earth to the witches' world.

Eli knew what she was witnessing, but she couldn't understand. Didn't *want* to understand.

"Its essence," she said. "It's … bleeding."

"This is what happened to the moon," said Circinae. "The Coven got greedy and stole all of its magic. Everything died. It's just an empty rock now. That's why we moved here."

Horror filled Eli's body, coursing through her veins like poison. "We're predators," she whispered, "eating worlds."

Circinae shook her head. "It wasn't supposed to be like this. Our world can't exist alone, but it can exist in harmony with other worlds — by sharing magic, by combining organic and inorganic materials, by adapting and evolving and changing. By dying. But the Coven learned how to live forever. They devour a world, drinking its essence, and then move on to another. But vengeance and hurt are sticky, and they follow us — they follow our magic. Sometimes the dead refuse to be left behind."

"Ghosts," breathed Eli.

"Yes. The City of Eyes has enchantments strong enough to keep them out. But Earth doesn't. That's what ghosts are — traces of the dead Moon people. Lost souls and spells and sorrow. *We* made the ghosts."

Eli's head was spinning. "And now the Coven is killing the Earth."

"They already have another galaxy in mind once they've destroyed this one. Your humans call it Andromeda."

"We have to stop them!"

"We can't." Circinae rolled a sugar cube around in her hand, fingertips glittering with the crystals. "It's too late, Eli. I've tried to keep you safe. Don't you understand? I've been trying to prove that your kind are still useful. I'm tired of watching my daughters being murdered." A tear slid down her face, leaving a streak of ash on her cheek.

Circinae will kill me, Eli had said.

It wouldn't be the first time, Kite had said.

Is that what Kite had discovered? That the Coven's past was littered with the bodies of dead daughters, broken or deficient tools? Did Kite know what the Witch Lord was doing to the world?

"I won't be useful in the new galaxy, you mean. They will need new tools — better daughters."

"I'm sorry, Eli."

"It's not too late." She turned to look at her mother. "We can stop them."

Another ashy tear slipped down Circinae's face. "No, daughter. We can't. They're already here."

Eli stepped away from her. "You called them."

"I had no choice."

"You're a murderer."

"I'm your mother."

"You're not my mother, witch." Eli pointed the truth blade at her. "I will renounce you. I will erase you. *I will undo you.*"

"Your blades won't work on me. I created you." But she didn't sound sure.

"It's not for you." Eli spun the blade so the handle was facing Circinae and the tip was pressed against her own chest.

Circinae stepped forward, the sugar on her nails hardening and growing, until long talons reached for her daughter. "Stop this. You are still useful. They might let you live. I could make modifications for the new planets, I could remake you, I could —"

Eli's harsh voice cut through Circinae's protest. "I erase you, I undo you. I undo you, I erase you. I erase you, I undo you."

"I was inducted into the third ring, Eli. They've been watching through my eyes for weeks! I didn't know at first. They knew the second you arrived — I couldn't stop them!"

Eli traded her frost knife for bone. "If I'm made from your body, does your body bleed when mine does? Does this hurt you?" She carved a red line into her forearm and drew a sharp intake of breath at the pain.

"Eli, stop!"

"Blood for blood. Bone for bone. I have no mother. I have no body. I am no one. *I am nothing.*" Drops of blood fell and sizzled on the platform. The knife glowed red.

She would keep her secrets in her blades and throw them into the abyss.

She would not betray her friends again.

She would not give anything more to the Coven.

She would not be their tool.

She drew another blade.

Bird talons wrapped around Eli's wrist. "I order you to stop!"

But Circinae had made her daughter well, and Eli could not be stopped. Hanging precariously between worlds, Circinae's magic was already stretched to its limit, and here, in between things, Eli was at her strongest. Eli wrenched herself free from Circinae's grasp and tore one of her talons off.

The sounds of Circinae keening in pain accompanied Eli's chant.

It was an aria of regret.

More cuts, more blood on the knives. Eli fell to her knees, weak from blood loss, and in her final act of consciousness, she threw her blades into the galaxy.

Maybe they would find their way to the wastelands and be buried forever.

Maybe they would fall to Earth and mark her human grave.

Maybe they would hang forever in the space in between.

"Eli!" Circinae grabbed her the moment she collapsed. The last thought Eli had before she lost consciousness was that she hoped her friends had escaped.

When the wings of the Coven arrived, Eli was awake, sitting on a platform in the sky, staring blankly at a dying world. Her hands were empty.

"You will come with us," said a voice magnified by power and history. It echoed through the universe and rattled her rib cage.

She looked up at the figure who stood before her, one hand staunching the flow of blood from her arm. Under Eli's skin, a thin vein of quartz glittered in the starlight.

Dark red armour like dried blood. The wings of an albatross. The smell of newly dug graves in soft wet soil. Reflected in the armour, Eli could see the eyes of all the unfortunate souls he had collected.

Beside the creature, a woman with bird talons for hands was weeping soundlessly, the black drops leaving watercolour streaks in the air.

A note of sacred power was regurgitated from his throat as he laid claim to the girl in the sky. "Eli."

Names have power.

Names ensnare us in a web of futures and pasts, in secrets and promises, in debts we spend our entire lives trying to pay.

Names can free us, or they can break us.

She cocked her head to one side and frowned, the blood warm and sticky on her hand.

"Who's Eli?"

Thirty-Six

Underneath her, a blue-and-white planet slowly bled to death, while all around her stars and planets and comets danced and fought and fell in love. The girl with no name stood. She felt the threat from the great wings and reached for her hips, her hand falling over a belt with many straps. What did her hands grasp for? They felt empty. A surge of fear lit up her body like a light switch turning on.

"Who are you? What do you want?"

"She's damaged," said the wings. "The Coven will not be pleased."

"I can remake her. I can —"

The wings extended to their full breadth. The girl could taste the sweetness of overripe magic like honey and rotting fruit. The woman stopped speaking and fell to her knees.

"Forgive us," she sobbed.

Even the girl knew that this creature could not bring forgiveness.

He opened his mouth, and bees poured out.

They buzzed furiously toward the girl. The girl kept her eyes open, even when they started stinging. It was only pain. The discarded bodies of the insects hung in the air like a prayer to death.

The woman, crouched on the ground in a pool of her own muddy tears, suddenly rose up, her desperation like a beacon in the dark. The girl's eyes shuttered and changed somehow, and she could see the redorange magic blazing under the skin of the witch and somehow understood that the skin-and-bone body was not her true form.

"There is only one way that bird mothers teach their daughters to fly," she said, "and it's your time to learn, little one." She walked into the cloud of pain and pushed the girl off the platform.

Air under her feet. Nothing to hold on to for years and years. Just empty space.

She was falling, or maybe flying.

Different strands of magic were already winding themselves around the woman who claimed to be her mother, until she was completely wrapped in the grip of the Coven. The girl watched as the magic hardened into the shell of a beehive, and then the woman was gone. As the girl floated away, the hive became smaller and smaller, until it was the size of a bee, and then disappeared entirely.

She was floating in space.

She turned her head to watch the bloody planet far away. Could she make it that far? Why was it dying?

Was she dying?

A rush of wings. The taste of graveyard dirt in her mouth.

The wings were coming for her.

She had nowhere to run, and no wings of her own to carry her. Her fingers were still twitching for a familiar weight. She opened her mouth and teeth spilled out, long and curved and thirsting for magic. The cuts on her arms had hardened into lines of granite. It would take the wings a long time to tear her body apart. The thought gave her grim satisfaction.

The stars started to sing.

Softly, gently, a lullaby of heat and light and hurt and love. A song of loneliness that cut the girl to the core. She understood loneliness. The music swelled in her body, brushing her clavicle. It sounded like home.

A blue girl appeared before her, and the song intensified.

I won't let them take you, the thought poured itself into the nameless one's mind.

Who are you? she thought back, but no one answered.

And then there were wings that cut through the fabric of time and space like a scalpel cuts through flesh, and the feathers were cutting into the blue girl.

The blue girl held up a single daisy as an offering. The petals wilted, one by one falling into the universe. They looked like snowflakes in the dark.

One stroke, one feather, and the severed head of the flower tumbled from the stalk. The blue girl shoved it in her mouth and chewed.

The wings didn't hesitate. They cut through the body of the blue girl. Her song of pain burst into life, and all the stars and planets brightened at her cry, as if they, too, were feeling her pain. Her body fell away like discarded wrapping paper. Her face was the last part of her to collapse, and the mouth spat out a gummy, saliva-covered, half-chewed flower.

A sun blazed into life. Aquamarine fire. The wings reared back, as if burned by its presence.

Go through the door.

The half-eaten flower punctured a hole in space, and through the gap, the girl could see the naked arms of trees.

I have to kill it.

The voice sounded remorseful, but the girl with no name felt no regret. Should she trust this strange creature, this little sun? The voice was familiar, and it soothed her soul. She felt its warmth and somehow that was enough. She reached for the doorway.

As she passed through, she could feel the heat of a sun that would incinerate anything that came too close. She looked back over her shoulder. The bluegreen essence was already regrowing a body, and the last thing the nameless one saw before she passed through the doorway was the pretty face of a blue girl eating the creature's head.

Thirty-Seven

Rock pressing against her spine. The necks of trees turning so the invisible eyes of the forest could watch her. The nameless one extended her lizard tongue to taste the air. It was heavy with salt. Her vision was blurry until she switched eyes, and then she could see strange auras around everything. It gave her a headache, so she switched back.

Someone brought her a pair of badly scratched glasses, and her vision improved. "Are you hurt?" A man with a drooping moustache and worry in his eyes reached for her. She hissed and showed her teeth. He drew back, eyes wide. "What's wrong?"

She was on all fours, crawling like the animal she was. He smelled like fear, and she wondered if he was her intended prey. She felt an overwhelming urge to kill.

"Why are you looking at me like that?" His voice wavered. "Eli?"

"Why is she taking so fucking long?"

The girl's attention was drawn to another person standing in shadow. They wore dark jeans and a leather jacket, and their hair was a shocking violet. Their arms were outstretched and their eyes were narrowed, facing the puncture in matter. Sweat dripped down their nose. The girl suddenly understood: they were keeping the doorway open.

A moment later, the blue girl fell through the tear and collapsed onto the island, her hair writhing like worms about to be stuck on a hook. "Close it," she gasped and then coughed up a handful of albatross feathers.

Purple Hair dropped their arms and the wound healed itself. They wiped the sweat from their face. "Jesus Christ, you took your damn time. What happened?"

"He would have told the Coven," said the blue girl, rising to her knees. She began to comb her hair with very long, very thin fingers.

"So he's dead?"

A secret smile. A voice like a secret. "He was delicious."

The nameless one lunged. Blue's essence flared up and knocked her down. "Bad girl," she chided.

"What's wrong with her?" said the man. "She looks like she's going to bite me."

"Oh, that," replied Blue, her hair mesmerizing in undulating waves. "She's lost her memory."

"What?!"

"Oh, don't worry, what's lost can be found again."

The nameless one listened to this exchange with interest as she stared up at the constellations overhead. She had been up there just moments ago, and this blue creature had saved her. That was something. Not enough for trust, but a start. Her eyes fell on the purple-haired human.

"You were using magic," she said.

"Yes."

"Humans can't use magic."

"Well, I can."

Pause.

"You seem useful."

"Thanks."

Something flickered under her rib cage. The girl with no name couldn't stop staring. There was something about them.

Who was this person to her? Did she want to find out? She stood up and stepped toward them. They flinched. She turned away, trying to ignore the warmth she felt from the proximity of their body. She looked out into the darkness, trying to read her past in the twisted branches and falling leaves. She found nothing.

"How do we get her memory back?" Purple Hair asked. "Kite, you must know something."

Kite. The name fit. A blue girl who could fly. She made a note of that.

Already, her mind was turning to revenge. Dreaming of feathers and blood and the drone of an army of sacrificial bees. "Who sent the wings?" she asked Kite. "That's who I want to kill."

"She hasn't changed that much, I see." The man tugged on his moustache and tried a floppy version of a smile.

"I don't know who you are, but if you want to live, you'll do what I tell you," she said. "I was built to survive, but I don't think you were."

"The Coven sent them," said Kite.

"*Your* people," Purple said pointedly.

Kite starting chewing on her hair. "*Our* people," said Kite.

"I'm missing something," said the girl, panic rising in her lungs. "My blades. We find them, then we kill the Coven."

"We have time," said Kite.

"We don't have time," said Purple.

She liked the feeling of dirt under her feet. She craved the taste of salt. She missed the weight of her blades around her hips. The bee stings were starting to itch.

"Can I peel my skin off like you did?" she asked Kite.

"Sorry, baby, no, you can't."

Kite had fought the wings and won. Purple Hair had opened a door. "What's he good for?" She nodded at the boy.

"Rude," he said.

"Making playlists," said Purple.

"True," he said. "But still rude."

"I don't know, love, but you brought them here," said Kite.

She wanted to ask why he was covered in stones, but she didn't. Asking too many questions was dangerous. Revealing yourself was dangerous. And she was going to use these creatures, somehow, to survive.

She took a moment to inspect her body — the cracks on her surface had all been filled by stone, and while she was covered in blood, she was no longer bleeding.

She started walking. She walked with such grace and care that she barely disturbed the water as she passed through it. Silent as a killer.

"Where are you going?!" he called after her, pebbles grinding against one another.

"The forest, of course."

The skeleton trees shook their limbs in warning as she passed.

Thirty-Eight

"Go into the forest," Circinae had said.

Her daughter, small for her age and disobedient for a made-thing, had watched her with unblinking black eyes.

"Go into the forest and bring me four leaves from the quietest tree."

Circinae had turned back to her knitting. When she looked up again, the girl was gone. Circinae hadn't heard a footstep. A slow smile unzipped itself from her mouth.

This was the one. She could tell.

Eli had gone barefoot into the forest, listening for the quietest tree. She was learning how to listen with her whole body. She still bore a scar on the sole of her left foot from stepping on a tree root that had turned out to be the shell of an invisible viper.

She had walked for hours, moving carefully through the deadly forest. She had found the tallest tree, the angriest tree, and the loneliest tree (she sat beside it for a while, just to keep it company), but she still hadn't managed to find the quietest tree. She was tired and hungry. "So many excuses," she could hear Circinae saying, "like a human child." That word, *human*, haunted her. Eli could not be human. She had to be better than human. She was witch-made.

Frustrated, Eli pressed a tight fist against the closest trunk, as if knocking gently. The roots underneath her feet began shifting like a writhing pile of snakes, and a pit opened up. Eli fell into the earth.

Dirt in her mouth. In her ears. In her *eyes*. Roots tangling themselves around her ankles.

It was so dark.

She couldn't breathe. *You don't always need to breathe*, she reminded herself. But the pain in her lungs still hurt, and there was no sun to touch her skin, nothing. The whisper of fear curled around her rib cage.

Mother will come, she thought. *She can always find you.*

(Once that had been a comfort.)

The roots tightened around her limbs and curled around her throat. Silt in her nostrils; the smell of mouldy leaves and dead worms.

Time passed.

Circinae didn't come.

Deep underground, Eli learned to make friends with her fear. To live in its thorns and smoothness, in its sharp pulse. She took that fear and made it into a weapon.

She gave it to the tree.

She pushed that trembling fear out of her body and into the roots.

The tree screamed.

As if in pain, it pulled its roots out of the earth. Eli clung to one and was dragged above ground. Kneeling on the ground, she coughed and coughed. She rolled over onto her back and looked up. The sky had never been so beautiful.

Then she dusted herself off and kept going.

Much later, she returned home, a dirty scrap of a girl clutching a few precious leaves. Fear hung like a murky halo around her body — not quite an enemy, not quite a friend.

Circinae said nothing about the fear or the filthy body. She put down her knitting, took the leaves from Eli, and breathed on them. They shimmered like glass. Then, with one talon, she scratched a few lines into the surface and chuckled to herself.

"Now," said Circinae, "you will learn to read."

She had forgotten who she was and who she loved, and hated, and why.

She hadn't forgotten the world.

Some memories go too deep to be removed.

"How do you know they're not in the junkyard?" the man asked.

Kite's sing-song voice cut across the space between them. "She buried herself. This is where things go to hide. The junkyard collects the lost, abandoned, and unwanted. Things forgotten through neglect or harm. If her blades are unbroken, they will be in the forest."

"And if they're broken?" Purple had caught up to them.

"Then they're broken," said Kite.

"Then I'll get revenge with my teeth," said the girl. "And I will choose a new name."

The sky had turned an anemic red, and the forest glowed pink under the pale light. Trees like goddesses towered over the four small bodies, their branches strung with glistening vines and fragrant moss as if adorned by jewels. All of the trees were one tree; all of the roots that wound through the soil and wrapped around stones and witches and lost assassins were one root. The forest was a single living, breathing ancient, with thousands of eyes and trunks and branches.

The magic was so thick that it crowded the girl's lungs and made her head swim. With her magic eyes, the girl could see the kaleidoscopic dance of magic and tenderness that existed between every leaf and branch. Even Kite was affected by the forest's fierce life force: her glow was stronger, blotting out her features, as if her essence was trying to escape the body she had chosen.

Head spinning, the nameless girl looked for the magic that was hers, the thread of shadow and light that tethered her blades to her body, the pathway that she could follow to regain her memories. She let the colours dance around her field of vision until she found it: the thread was black and glittered like morning dew, like the dying planet. She felt a twinge of panic when she thought about the world she had witnessed slowly being executed. She told herself it didn't matter. What mattered was survival, strength, and power. What mattered was getting her blades back, and then taking revenge.

She followed the thread.

Her companions spoke in hushed voices, and she learned their names. She wondered again who these people were to her. Why they seemed to care about her. Assassins worked best alone.

Leaves fell in their wake, marking a path in gold and red. Archways of moss studded with offerings of rosehips and rusted bicycle wheels hung overhead. Kite paused every few steps to wind strands of hair around branches. Tav paused before an altar of tangled roots and pearlescent fungi. They took out one of their silver earrings and set it under a glowing mushroom.

"Just feels right," they said when they caught Cam staring. After a moment, Cam shuffled over and offered a flaking piece of mica to the altar.

The girl kept walking. She didn't have time to worship the forest, and she didn't have anything to give.

They hadn't gotten far when the scent of smoke and sacrifice poured into the grove. A strange shadow flickered overhead. In the distance, a single lidless eye seemed to watch them.

A tree was burning.

The girl clutched at her wrist, feeling the fire in the hawthorn-laced contours of her bones. Thick purplegrey smoke spilled like a sickness over the trees. The forest shook its magnificent mane in fury, and leaves rained down.

"This is wrong," said the girl. "I can feel it."

"Fire is forbidden here," said Kite, her hair whipping around her face. "Even the children would not risk it."

"That's not our mission," said Tav.

"The Coven should know about this," said Kite. "The Witch Lord will be furious." Her voice trembled, and the girl with no name wondered what kind of creature could inspire such fear in the girl of salt, the girl who had devoured the red wings.

A piercing sound broke through the quiet and spread from tree to tree. The forest was screaming.

Kite's body was starting to flicker, becoming less solid and defined. The nameless one could see the shape of vines and flowers through her flesh.

"I'm sorry," Kite whispered and immediately vanished.

The girl watched in confusion as the glittering threads that bound her to her knives were joined by other threads that led to the burning tree. Kite was gone, but the girl knew how to find her. All she had to do was follow the strands of golden light that stretched between their bodies, threads that followed Kite deep into the forest. As she watched the magic flow between bodies, she understood that she was entering a web of connections and feelings.

They drew her to Tav. To Cam. She knew somehow that they stretched all the way to the City of Ghosts.

She hesitated before flipping to her yellow eyes and grinding her teeth. "She's gone to save the tree. We have to go after her."

"It could be a trap," said Tav. "We need to get your knives first."

The girl with no name offered a lazy smile. "You think I'm only dangerous with my blades and my memory?" She showed off her canines. "You don't have to follow me. Just don't get in my way."

When they found her, Kite had rematerialized behind a grove of silver poplars. The bluegreen light that flowed under her skin was flickering like a flame. She was staring through the slender branches and trembling, her light wavering. Eli looked through the arms of the poplars.

Someone stood under a giant elm, basking in the glow of the fire. Her hands were pressed against the trunk, forcing heat into its body. Silverblack bark was curling and burning to ash.

Pearl tears dripped down Kite's face as she spoke. "She's a member of the Coven. I didn't know it had gone this far. I can't touch her. I can't stop her."

"A member of the Coven," said the girl. "An enemy."

"A witch," said Tav.

"Great magic requires great sacrifice," whispered Kite. "But who would risk killing the forest? What are they doing?"

The girl reached out and caught a few pearls as they fell from Kite's eyes. She tossed one in the air and caught it. "It's time to kill a witch." She smiled at Tav.

"Have you killed one before?"

"I can't remember."

They both laughed.

The nameless one felt the anticipation of the hunt rising in her throat and pooling under her collarbone. She swallowed one of the pearls and felt her senses heighten. She reached out to touch a strand of magic and felt it tremble under her hand.

The witch felt the vibration and pulled back from the tree. The screaming stopped.

The girl with no name grinned at Tav and then walked out of the shadow and into the light.

"Who sent you?" said the witch, frowning. "Whose daughter are you?"

"No one's," she said.

"Good." Flames burst from the witch's hands. A girl made of hawthorn should be careful of fire. The girl placed another pearl in her mouth and cracked it open. The flame split around a body that smelled like an ocean. Kite's tears kept her safe.

Suddenly, the girl lunged, scratching out with fingernails turned to claws. The witch vanished and reappeared behind her.

Two hunters circled one another.

More leaves fell, until the trees around them were bare, and the ground was barely visible.

The girl lunged again, this time crouching low, her bite piercing the skin of the witch's leg. The witch didn't fall back. Instead, she touched the girl.

This time, the flame caught, singeing her hair and numbing her entire left arm. She rolled away, fumbling for a pearl. When the girl's tooth cracked the surface, a feeling of coolness washed over her and soothed the burn. But the witch was already reaching for her, the hand promising fire and pain.

A body appeared, crusted with limestone and shale and quartz, shielding the girl. Protecting her. *Cam.*

Stone doesn't burn. The witch hesitated for a moment, and that was her undoing. Tav stepped out from behind the elm and pressed a hand against the witch's back. The body tore open, the witch's essence bleeding out. The wound spread from Tav's palm like a sickness across the witch's body, until the essence hardened and shattered into pieces. The witch collapsed into a pile of white ash.

The girl wondered if she had ever seen a witch die before. It was beautiful.

Kite was weeping soundlessly, strands of seaweed sticking to her face, tiny shells tumbling to the forest floor.

"Thank you," the girl turned to Cam. "You saved me."

"I guess I am good for something after all," gasped Cam. "I thought the witch was going to kill me." He shuddered.

Tav was staring at their palm, an indecipherable expression on their face. The girl could hear their rapid heartbeat and felt the heat rising in their body. From fear or excitement?

"You opened a door in her body," said the girl. "You tore her essence apart. Thank you for killing her."

Tav looked up, curling their hand into a fist. "I didn't mean to. I just saw the magic inside her, and I reached out and ... and made her stop." The fist dropped to their side. "I've never killed anyone before."

"You get used to it."

"Do I want to get used to it?" Their eyes were bright as two suns.

"If you want to survive." She met their gaze, but Tav turned way.

"What was the witch doing here, anyway?" Tav asked Kite, whose tears had dried up.

Kite shook her head, hair lying limp and flat. "Nothing good."

"What does that mean?"

"It means they were using the life force from the tree for some kind of magic. Big magic. Forbidden magic."

They all turned to the tree. Already the bark was beginning to regenerate, the dead skin falling to the earth. The sap veins underneath pulsed with golden light. In the distance, another tree lit up with a golden light. And then another.

"It wants us to follow," said Kite.

The girl let the blackness slowly fill her eyes and found that the glittering black thread of her own magic lead in the same direction as the golden glowing trees.

"They're helping," she said.

They followed the golden trees until they came to a great oak tree, its roots shaping a small cavern.

"I've been here before." Her hand remembered the texture of its bark, the smell of lemon zest and iron.

"It sheltered us once, when we needed it." Kite rubbed her face against the trunk. "When we were hiding from the red wind. It protects its own."

"You say that like I belong here," said the girl.

Kite turned her jellyfish eyes on the assassin. "You belong everywhere."

Inside the cavern, wound tightly by roots and blanketed by leaves, were seven blades. At the girl's touch, the tree released them.

"I need to do this on my own. It's personal."

"Call us if you need anything," said Tav, worry in their eyes.

She nodded. They respected her privacy. They left the nameless one alone with her past.

She stared at the knives, the tools of an assassin. Something in her body called out to them, welcomed them, needed them. She ran one finger along glass and felt soothed deep in her bones.

She bent over, hesitated, and then licked the blade. It tasted of dirt and salt and bitter cranberry. It tasted of *her*. A spark twitched her tongue and with it came a name, although not her own — *Circinae. Mother. Maker. Tyrant.* A house with a door of charcoal and ash. Cinnamon sticks and sugar cubes. A hand, pushing her into the darkness.

Making her fly. The glass blade brought the home that was also a prison into sharp relief. She wondered if she should mourn the lost mother who, in her own way, had tried to save her. But she could not.

She drew back, and the words and images and feelings stopped. There was a tiny cut on the tip of her tongue, although the flat of the blade had been dull. She understood then that some of these memories would hurt. Did she really want them back?

Bracing herself, she picked up a different blade, the frost blade, and licked it. It was cold as ice and burned to the touch. This blade held Kite: desire, loss, sorrow. Blood and bones and revelry. The feelings she had for the Children's Lair — of grudging respect, of wariness — became illuminated in these memories. She understood that not all memories were needful, but she took them back into her body just the same. She drank the memories from the blade.

Pearl: the taste of fresh coffee and the glow of fluorescent lights. The abandoned stones and hair barrettes in the junkyard that spoke of a damaged bond between human and magic worlds. Great winged beasts and shadows that came to life. The essence of the world that was physical and intangible, feeling and body all at once.

Thorn: every ghost she had ever killed returned to her, and the memories, once bright with satisfaction, were now dull with guilt over the death of the human and the threat to Tav. And behind each ghost was now the knowledge of their own pasts — lost souls from the moon, a people who had lost their home and their lives to the witches' hunger. Wandering mouths, thirsty for revenge or home, who had found their way to Earth.

Stone: the lingering touch of the forest that saw itself as a protector even as its embrace could harm. The days and nights she spent trapped underground, or in the tallest tree, learning to survive. The feeling of safety on the island or in the Labyrinth. Shelter.

Obsidian: hunger, death, power. A blade that could kill even witches. How had they trusted her with it? Because she had been their tool, and never a threat. Until now. She found herself back in the chamber of the Coven with the floating heads and the painful whiteness of the walls. She found herself full of rage — at herself, at her mother, at the world that made her and used her and discarded her. She was angry, and that anger was life-giving. It was powerful. She could use it. She remembered that feeling of belief, of knowing she had a place. She remembered it, and she rejected it. She had changed, and the blade had changed with her. It understood.

She saved the bone blade for last. She had drunk most of her memories now. If any were missing, had spilled from the blade and her mind, then they were gone, and there would be no retrieving them. That didn't bother her. She had enough.

She placed the last blade to her tongue and tasted smoke. She knew immediately that this knife contained her name. (The bone blade, the tracker, remembered many names, but its own more than anything.)

Names held power.

She had not chosen her own name.

Once she took this final memory into her body, that name would be re-given to her, relearned, imprinted on her body.

And now she knew who had named her, who had made her, had claimed ownership over her. But she also knew she had grown into the name, had made a home in it, had made it her own. This time, she would choose the name. She would choose the pain of having a mother, the fear of living under the Coven's gaze. The willfulness of turning away from a future of obedience and toward something unknown and dangerous.

It was, in the end, her name, and no one else's. She drank the final memories.

Eli sheathed the knives and stood.

She had work to do.

But first — Eli raised the bone blade and cut a handful of hair. Then she carefully wove it around the gnarled roots of the oak.

Thirty-Nine

They were waiting for her in a grove of cedars nearby. She followed their scents. Kite was humming to herself, hair and skirts fluttering around her body. Cam was rubbing a piece of limestone on his neck. Tav's hands were in their jean pockets, their face grim.

Eli met Tav's gaze and felt a flush of shame. She remembered standing over their body. That moment when she thought it might be easier if she forgot everything she had learned since meeting them, if she pretended Tav was a ghost. If she let herself be a tool.

How could they welcome her back, after what she had almost done?

"Did it work?" Cam looked up eagerly. "Do you remember me?"

"I remember that you drive like an old man."

A smile split across his face. "Too bad," he said. "I was hoping I could tell you all my jokes again."

Tav raised their chin and walked forward.

"Tav —"

"You're not my keeper, Cam. Stay out of it."

He fell silent. Kite watched curiously.

When they were close enough to touch, Tav stopped. "You remember who I am?"

Eli nodded.

"I don't know where the Coven got my deadname from, but I don't want to hear you say it. That's not me, understand?"

"I understand, Tav."

They exhaled. "Still want to finish your mission?"

Dark eyes. Gold ring around the pupils. Eli didn't look away. "Now's my chance, I guess. If I wanted to."

"Yeah. Is that what you want?" Their voice was light, casual — but it was a challenge, and Eli was mesmerized by the fire in their eyes as they stared down the assassin who had been sent to take their life as punishment for daring to have magic.

"Spoken like a witch," she said admiringly.

"Spoken like a human," Tav corrected. "You should give us more credit."

"You're right. Spoken like a human." Eli reached for her belt. When she raised the obsidian blade, Tav didn't even flinch.

Eli spun it around and offered the hilt to them.

Tav reached out and took it. Eli held her breath. But this time, the blade did not cut or burn the magical part of Tav. This time, the blade rested in their hand, perfectly balanced across the lifeline of their palm. It looked like it belonged there.

Her hand fell across her other knives, a habit she had used to soothe herself since she was a child. The blades were warm to the touch.

"Are you sure?"

"Can't leave you unprotected again. You get into so much trouble without me."

"Says the girl who nearly got herself killed." Tav's thumb slid across the shaft of the knife, and Eli could feel the gentle touch somewhere under her clavicle. She shivered.

"Helps to have backup."

For a moment, they stood in silence, staring at the sliver of volcanic glass.

She didn't say, *It's a part of me.*

She didn't say, *I trust you to keep it safe.*

Tav knew. Eli could tell by the look in their eyes, and the careful way their fingers wrapped around the hilt. They knew.

So instead, she said, "Don't lose it. It's hard to replace."

Tav grinned. "I'll try not to."

Leaves rained down on them, gold and green and scarlet tipped with bronze. The leaves brushed their shoulders and faces and fell to the forest floor in a carpet of colour and life and promise. Tav reached forward and picked a leaf out of Eli's hair. They twirled it once and then released it into the air.

Somewhere, on another planet, there were other trees thirsting for the sun, their deep roots arching under the soil. There was life.

The image of the bleeding Earth blotted out Eli's vision until all she could see was the steady stream of black essence flowing into the galaxy as the witches drank the life force of the world that half claimed her. The world that had made Tav and Cam. A planet with a life of its own. And every second Eli stood here was a moment closer to Earth's death.

"What?" Tav caught the shifting mood as deftly as a prism catches the light.

Eli swallowed, throat tight, vocal cords clouded with fear. She could feel rose petals wilting in her sternum.

"There's something I need to tell you," she said. "All of you."

Horror crept through the party as Eli relayed what she had seen.

"The entire planet?" said Cam, struggling to make sense of the scale of the threat. "All of it?"

"That must be why all the witches are fleeing Earth," said Tav. "I wonder if the Hedge-Witch knows." They fell silent, lost in their thoughts.

Kite crooned a quiet song that tasted of ice floes and algae.

"Did you know about this?" Eli turned to the girl with hands like water.

Her pale, pupil-less eyes glowed with an alien light. "I found traces," she said, fingers rippling in midair. "In the archives. Mentions of moon people and a civilization of light. I don't know what happened to them. I didn't know they were ghosts. If those memories were written down, they have been lost or destroyed." She bowed her head in mourning — although for the dead moon people or the loss of a precious book, Eli didn't know.

Silence fell like a shroud. Even the golden rays that spilled over the branches felt cold and empty. Tav broke the tension, eyes flashing with righteous anger.

"The Heart."

Cam looked up. "You think —"

"I think the Heart is the key. If we steal the Heart, they can't hurt Earth anymore. They won't have any power."

"Will that heal —"

"I don't know!" Tav tugged at their hair in frustration. "But look — if we have the source of magic, we can do whatever we want, right? We can stop the Coven. We can save Earth."

We can power a revolution, thought Eli. *We can break and remake the world.* As she stared at Tav, she could almost see the faint outline of charcoal wings emerging from powerful shoulder blades. Eli could see them at the head of an army, turning cities to ash.

Could the human world handle that kind of power?

Kite's hair was trembling, and her bluegreen glow dimmed. "You want our Heart?" She turned to Eli. "What will that do to our world?"

"I don't know, but they're right," Eli found herself saying. She didn't meet Tav's eyes. She was afraid of what she would see in them. "Stealing the Heart won't stop the witches, but it will hurt them. And if we can learn how to use it — well, maybe we can stop this. Without it, we aren't strong enough to go up against the Coven. This is our best chance."

"Now?" Kite whispered to herself. "Is it time? Already?" Her skirts pooled around her feet like water. "I thought we would have more time."

"We don't have time," said Eli. "We have to get to the Coven."

Everyone started speaking over one another.

"If we go back to the Labyrinth —"

"I could try opening a door —"

"The risk —"

Kite sang an arpeggio with a clear, strong voice. The others turned to her in surprise.

"If it's time, then I can help," she said softly. "I am the Heir. I will take you to the Coven."

Eli narrowed her eyes. After everything they had been through together, she still wasn't sure if she should trust Kite. "Aren't you still under a compulsion?"

"That ended when the pine needle entered your body," said Kite gently. "Or I would not have been able to save you from the wings of the Coven."

"If you can take us to the Coven, why didn't you tell us earlier?" The stones on Cam's chest scraped against one another.

Kite stared at him and slowly began to chew on her hair.

"Can you take us to the Heart?" Tav pressed.

"I don't know," said Kite. "The Coven — the place, not the witches' council — usually brings me to the library. I think it likes that there is someone who cares about its history."

Eli's hand reached for obsidian and stumbled over the empty sheath. "If you take us to the Witch Lord …"

Kite let her hands drop to her sides and turned slowly to face Eli. She tilted her head to one side, exposing her throat. "Will you use your teeth?" she asked lightly. "I've always wanted to see that."

"No, you don't." Cam shuddered.

Kite smiled. "I've always loved monsters."

"You've always loved power." But her words lacked bite. Kite had saved her when she could have thrown her to the Coven. Eli had to trust that she meant what she said. Eli checked her blades one last time.

Tav was watching her. "We have to do this," they said. "Let her help us."

No one disagreed with them, although Eli was troubled by the eager gleam in their eyes.

"Okay," she said finally. "Take us to the Coven."

Kite applied glamours to the humans. They would enter as servants, glowing dimly, imitating the radiant magic that flowed from every witch. No one expected servants to have strong magic, so the illusion should be enough. No one looked too closely at servants, those who failed to ascend to seats of power, as if that failure might be contagious.

It was the perfect disguise.

"Killing a world takes time and power," said Kite. "Draining that much life force. Perhaps that's why ..."

Eli could see the burning tree in her eyes. Power requires sacrifice. Power requires risk. Was the Coven willing to desecrate sacred ground in their hunger to devour Earth?

"How long before the Coven starts devouring its own?" Eli asked.

Kite twitched, and her body became more transparent. She didn't want to think about the threat to her own world.

"The tree —"

"Yes." Tears glittered in Kite's eyes. "The tree. It seems the Coven is not only sacrificing daughters and lesser witches to increase their power. They will use anything and anyone in the worlds."

There was nothing else to say.

The mood was sombre, but with an undercurrent of anticipation. Eli felt the familiar stab of adrenalin. Tav's fingertips played piano scales on the obsidian knife. The stones on Cam's body trembled against one another, a grating sound that made Eli clench her teeth. Only Kite seemed calm and placid, hair undulating gently around her cheekbones.

Eli had no glamour on — she was going as herself. It was a risky plan: Kite escorting the assassin, as if to present her as a gift to the upper ring of the Coven. It might fool the lower rings, but if the Witch Lord appeared … well, Kite's royal blood could only take them so far. Traitors didn't exist in the City of Eyes. They were fed to the Coven.

"We could do this without you," said Kite. "I could —"

"Enough." Eli's voice was harsh and gravelly. "I'm not staying behind." Sleeplessness made her eyelids twitch, and her eyes shuttered between sets uncontrollably, black bleeding over yellow, only to drain away again.

"I can make you a glamour for that." Kite gestured at her eyes.

"No. We get in, we get the Heart, and we get out. We try to avoid an altercation with the first ring, but if it happens, I'll distract them while Tav makes a door. And whatever happens — don't wait for me."

Cam opened his mouth to argue, but the look in Eli's eyes made him stop. Kite raised her arms, and a funnel of water rose from the river around her body. When she released it, droplets of water glittered brilliantly in her hair. She held her head high, eyes like frost. Eli sucked in a breath. For the first time, she truly felt that she was in the presence of the Heir.

"At least we have our invincible assassin back." Cam nudged Tav.

"No one's invincible."

Kite spoke a single word, her tone low and seductive with power.

A moment later, they stood on the Coven steps. As Kite walked toward the painfully bright building, a door appeared, and behind it, Eli glimpsed a single hallway.

Eli entered the Coven for the last time.

Forty

Once, when Eli was still a child, Kite had taken her into the library. The magical archives housed all the history and memory that most witches tried to forget.

But the stone walls of the Coven remembered. Everything was alive in the City of Eyes, and the walls and turrets and passages of the witch stronghold were no exception. It had a mind of its own. Not even the Witch Lord had been able to bury the past completely — although she had tried. And despite being sealed away, burned, hidden, and drowned, the library remained. Only Kite was allowed to read the forbidden histories. Only Kite, an extension of the Witch Lord's power, who would use this knowledge for her mother's gain. No one else was trusted in the chamber of blasphemies.

Kite cared for the library with love.

Eli was made for destruction, for forgetting, for moving forward. She didn't look back. She had never understood Kite's obsession with old tomes and lost languages. Eli was life, furious and bright and brutal. The past was death.

"I want to give you a secret," Kite had breathed in her ear. "Come with me."

Children thrive on secrets.

So Eli had followed, even when Kite took her into the Coven, a space the little assassin was forbidden from entering except when summoned by the first ring.

They were breaking the rules. But Eli trusted Kite, and so she followed.

That day, the library had shaped itself into a large cavern, with books like gemstones glittering in rock. Stalactites dripping ink speared from the low ceiling, and stalagmites stabbed upward like a gate.

Eli had reached out and caught a drop of ink as it fell from the longest, sharpest point in the room. Searing pain. The smell of charred flesh. When she drew back, a scar in the shape of an ink blot marked her palm. Steam rose from her hand.

"I wasn't made of this," she said, eyes flashing black. "The magic here is alive." She stepped in front of Kite as if to protect her, drawing her glass blade to reflect malevolent magic.

"Don't," said Kite.

The entire cavern had groaned, a sound like stone scraping on metal. Pages fell from the ceiling, folding themselves until they were only jagged edges with barely legible lines of print.

Eli tore the pages apart with one swift motion. Ink bled down her blades. Kite had begun moaning a mournful melody of sorrow and fear.

"Don't," Kite whispered again.

Eli should have known better than to fight the very building of the Coven. Kite should have known better than to bring a wild animal into her home.

It happened fast. Eli tore through fibre and leather with thorn and glass, but the library was old and powerful. Within moments, Eli was buried under a landslide of books and rubble.

She never cried out, not once. She had been trained well.

Smoke and sparks filled the room, ink and blood pooling over the floor. Eli was being suffocated by the weight of paper.

"Please," Kite asked the room. "I won't bring her again." She had wept salt to soak up the ink. Her hair whipped around her face like a hurricane, showing her distress.

When Eli was finally freed, covered in lacerations and burn marks, Kite led her gently out of the room. Eli had never gone back to the library.

They were coming for the Heart.

A thrill darted through Eli's nervous system, senses heightened by the danger and promise of pain. This was a different kind of hunt, but a hunt nonetheless.

Their footsteps made no sound. The hallway seemed to go on forever, and the eerie silence made them uncomfortable. Only Kite seemed unmoved by the strangeness of the Coven, walking through the halls as if she owned them.

Maybe she did.

The hall ended abruptly, and they entered a large room overflowing with thick tomes and dusty letters. Heavy curtains studded with paper moths lined the walls, and the ceiling was so high up Eli couldn't see where it ended. A place where words could cut and history refused to stay buried. A place that had rejected her. The library.

"Kite." Eli's voice was a warning.

"I want you to show us," she said.

"I already told you."

Cam cleared his throat. "I don't really understand what you told us."

"I'd like to see," said Tav, watching Eli closely. "Please?"

Eli sighed. "Okay. But we have to do this fast. We're running out of time."

"You keep saying that." Kite smiled indulgently. "But we have a few more moments before everything is destroyed."

Kite cleared a space on the floor and opened a large tome of gardening spells written out in elaborate curlicue handwriting. She waved her hand at the words, and the ink crawled off the paper until only an empty page was left behind. Eli knelt down, the ancient dust pricking through her jeans.

Even the dust knew she didn't belong here, among secrets and myths and knowledge. It was forbidden to her. She hesitated and then drew the bone blade, the tracker. The blade that always remembered.

A rustle of paper filled the space. Eli turned and saw the paper moths fluttering wildly.

"They're afraid of the knife," explained Kite. "Don't stray from the page and they won't harm you."

Eli nodded. She pressed the tip against the page, and ink soaked up through the paper. As her hand moved, dragging the tip across the paper, thick black lines traced the shape of the planet and the contour of each wound. When the drawing was complete, Eli took out the frost blade. She pressed the flat of the blade against the image and the scene came dizzyingly, wildly to life. Then she drew back.

Before them was the scene she had witnessed standing in the space between planets. Her breath caught in her throat. The bone blade had pulled the memory from her body, and the frost blade had sharpened its truth to a deadly weapon. Its aim was true. Cam inhaled sharply. Kite's eyes glowed more brightly, shining and wet, polished by pain. Tav stared at the drawing for a long time.

"I see now," whispered Kite, turning her luminous orbs on Eli. "We have so much to do."

"If we steal the Heart, it will weaken the Witch Lord's power. It should slow the bleeding. That's why we have to go *now*."

Cam was muttering under his breath. "Jesus fucking Christ. Holy fuck, oh my god, Jesus."

"Those wounds," said Tav. "Those are the seams between worlds. Like the one we used to cross."

"Yes," said Eli.

"Even when the tear seems to have closed, it's draining the Earth's energy."

"Yes."

Tav tapped their finger against the hilt of the obsidian knife. They looked up at Eli. "The flow of magic between things doesn't have to be hurtful, does it?"

"What do you mean?"

"These tears, or holes or whatever, are hurting the world because the power only flows one way, right?"

"Right. They're draining the life force of Earth. I told you that already. Look, we have to go." Eli felt exasperation tingling down her spine. And even though she had put away her knives, she could feel the library's intense dislike and mistrust of her, as thousands of books watched and waited.

"But *you* can travel both ways," Tav tapped the centre of the page, where the widest chasm had been depicted: the Vortex. The killing blow. "What if it wasn't a hole. What if it was a door?"

Eli stared at them. "A door," she repeated. Her eyes widened. "If you opened the door, the magic would flow both ways."

"And the planet would heal."

"How would we …" her voice trailed off. The look of fervour had returned to Tav's face. She already knew the answer to her question: only the Heart could power that kind of transformation.

And only Tav had the power to make doors.

Forty-One

Kite pressed her palm against the horror sketched out before them. The ink drained back to the pages it had been borrowed from. Then she took a moment to coax the floral handwriting back into the book. Once in place, the letters quivered slightly, as if they could feel the texture of death in the fibres of their home.

"Do you think you could?" asked Eli, hands twisting around the hilt.

"I don't know." Tav's eyes shone, and Eli was reminded of her vision of black feathers.

"You haven't tried."

"I know that."

"You could do more damage."

Tav laughed shortly. "I think now is the time to take a few risks, don't you?"

"What are you talking about?" Cam interrupted. He was rubbing a piece of marble that lived in the webbing between his thumb and pointer finger.

The sound of rustling grew louder. The paper moths were coming.

"My loves don't want you here," said Kite. "You can understand why they aren't quick to trust, after the way they've been treated."

Eli shivered, remembering the taste of ink in her throat and the weight of history on her chest. She had broken three ribs, and Kite had not spoken to her for weeks.

"Tav thinks they can close the doors," she said simply. "I think they're crazy."

"My therapist says you aren't supposed to call people crazy," said Cam.

"I'd rather be crazy than a ghost," said Tav. "That's what will happen to us if Earth dies."

Ink began falling from the sky. A storm was brewing.

Kite stood, her body pulsing with a clear aquamarine light. "Stay close, and the Coven will guide us."

"It's dangerous," said Eli.

Irritation coarsened Tav's tone. "I *know* that, what do you think —"

"And if *you* die —"

"Oh, I get it, *you're* the only one allowed —"

The library melted away.

Silence fell like a guillotine. They were back in the hallway, closing their eyes against the piercing whiteness. The hallway itself was keeping them silent, forcing the sounds to stay in their bodies. They followed Kite, who kept one hand on the wall and whispered to it; she seemed to be, in turns, cajoling and threatening the ancient building.

The hallway ended abruptly, and they found themselves in a chamber glowing with hatred and malice.

"No," whispered Eli, the chamber allowing the fear in her voice to be heard. Her knees locked. She had stood here too many times to count.

The floating heads.

The prodding fingers.

The death warrants that had passed through this space.

Eli had allowed herself to be their tool. A tear threatened to spill down her cheek, but she took a breath and kept moving through the empty chamber. Cam's hand on her shoulder helped.

They passed through dark rooms filled with venomous plants spitting acid, golden halls that moaned, vast chambers filled with diamond insects suspended in the air. Finally, the rooms collapsed back into a hallway, but it was now stained a sickly greenblack and smelled of infection.

"Here." Kite stopped. Her hair floated around her head, like antennae smelling the air. "I've never been here before."

Someone stepped out of the shadows, and Eli stifled a scream.

If the body had a face, it had been worn away with sun and wind and rain. A smooth blank head on a smooth blank body. It moved so gracefully that Eli felt like a clumsy mechanical object in comparison. She had never seen anyone move so fast, as if swimming through the air. As if every step was part of a complicated dance.

She knew, in that moment, her destiny: to fight this creature, and perhaps to die.

"I am the Guardian," said the faceless one. "I protect what is inside, and I protect what is outside. Turn back or die."

Kite had become immaterial, and through her body, Eli watched the creature prowl back and forth. Tav drew the obsidian blade. Cam stepped forward.

"No," said Eli. "This is my fight."

"It's all of our fight," said Tav.

"You can't win," Kite whispered.

Ignoring all of them, Eli walked *through* Kite, faced the Guardian, and then bowed. "It will be my honour to duel you."

"It has been a long time since these halls held honour," it said and bowed in return. And then it leaped.

Her superhuman reflexes kicked in, and Eli spun to one side, slashing wildly with the blade of thorns. Her blade cut through the air, and then the Guardian was on top of her.

An arm knocked the blade from her hand, and Eli was flung back against the wall, forcing the breath from her lungs. She cursed her human half and lunged again.

This time, she managed to plunge the bone blade into its shoulder before the Guardian threw her down the corridor. She landed on her arm and could hear the snap of bone cracking. Adrenalin spiked in her body, and she felt no pain, only pure undiluted rage. When she looked up, she could see her knife still embedded in its shoulder, black sand leaking from the body.

Drawing glass and pearl, she flung herself at it again.

It was learning her movements and easily blocked her strike. The Guardian wrenched the glass from her hand and crushed it.

Eli screamed in agony. It felt like losing a limb. Forcing herself to keep moving, she managed to evade its next attack and stabbed upward with the pearl blade.

The Guardian caught her unbroken arm and threw her to the ground. "You will die and be grateful for this mercy." It raised both arms to crush her skull.

Eli, looking up at this superior creature, wondered if Circinae knew that she had failed to make the perfect weapon. Lying in defeat, she watched the end come. She would die with dignity. She would face death with her eyes wide open.

"No!"

The sound of stone on stone crashed against Eli's ears. Cam had thrown himself in front of her, using his body as a shield. Tav threw themselves on the Guardian's back and plunged the obsidian dagger through the flesh and into the spirit that animated it. The Guardian screamed.

Eli suddenly felt cool, and a bluegreen glow covered her body. Kite was using her essence to heal her. The healing hurt, and Eli hovered at the edge of consciousness, forcing herself to stay awake, watching Cam and Tav put themselves in death's path for her.

When her eyes came back into focus, Eli saw that the Guardian was leaking black sand in two places. Cam was shaking but still standing. Several stones had been ripped from his body and lay shattered on the floor. Blood ran down Tav's nose. And still they stood between Eli and the Guardian. They were strong, but it was stronger. They were buying her time to escape, had chosen to sacrifice themselves for a made-thing, a killer, a tool.

Something awoke in Eli's body, and she sat up suddenly, gasping for breath. Her eyes were pure black. Her jaw was overflowing with teeth. Her blades started to shake.

The entire chamber shook with violence, as Eli was swept up in the dance of death, moving gracefully around her companions and grasping at the smooth skin of the Guardian. In one swift motion, Eli ripped the head from its body. The body fell, cracking into a million pieces.

Its face spoke, "I tried to guard you. Now you will suffer."

It crumbled into pieces of loose rock.

Forty-Two

Cam pulled her up. "You okay?"

"I look better than you."

He grinned. "I told you I'm handy in a fight,"

"First time for everything," said Tav.

Eli looked down at what remained of the Guardian. She reached down, retrieved the bone blade, and sheathed it.

"I'm sorry," she whispered, fingertips grazing a piece of stone.

She looked up at the doorway that had opened when the Guardian fell. She could see nothing through the darkness. The smell of the sacred infected in the air, and they all felt the itch of the forbidden.

This is what they had come for. This moment. This room. Eli took a breath, her adrenalin-ruined body begging for rest. *Not here. Not now.* Eli picked up the thorn blade from where it had fallen. She stared for a long moment at the pieces of glass that were scattered across the hallway. Some broken things could not be mended. She curled her hands into fists. Took another breath. Turned to her companions.

"Ready?"

The others nodded. Bracing herself, Eli led them into the unknown.

The walls were black, glittering with a hundred thousand flecks of mica and magic and old roots from trees that bloomed silver after every death. Above them, cathedral archways and Gothic spires and stone gargoyles intertwined in a tangle of styles and times and barbed-wire threats. It had begun as an idea, a thought in a powerful witch's mind. It had grown into a shape, a space, a floor. A powerful secret. A weapon.

In the centre of the cavern was a tree.

The tree was glowing with life and magic and purpose. It was honey and anglerfish and the memory of comets streaking endlessly across a clear night sky. It was black flame and birthday candles. Lightning and dying embers. A thousand different lights flickered across the ancient tree, tracing delicate veins and arteries under the bark. They had found the living, beating core of the world.

They had found the Heart.

But something was wrong. Eli could hear it in the scattered stones like fallen stars, the malevolence blooming from the spires like ink in water. She could taste the power here — it was old and malicious — and knew that these spells hadn't been designed to keep her out.

They were keeping someone *in*.

"It's a prison," said Eli.

Kite was glowing like a jellyfish, her brightness pulsing to the rhythm of the Heart. The stones that covered Cam's body were twinkling, catching and holding the light. The silver of mica powder on his skin glittered until he looked like a small galaxy. Even Tav's hair was lit up, an electric violet. And all the fault lines of Eli's making — the line under her kneecaps, a knuckle, the tendons on her left ankle — were glowing, too, as if bathed in moonlight.

They walked closer to the Heart. Leaves unfurled, sparks shimmering around their edges. Crystalline dewdrops fell from each leaf, shattering silently on the earth.

"So much pain." Kite was shaking, her hair wet and flat against her back. Water dribbled from each strand and flowed down her skirts.

"How —" Tav's voice failed.

"How do we carry it?" asked Cam, and Eli knew he didn't just mean, *How do we steal the Heart with our human hands and limited bodies?* but *How do we carry the weight of this power and pain, the source of all magic?* It would drown them. It would burn them up. It was like asking how to carry a star. It was impossible.

The smell of sulphur and aspartame. Wax dripping from the cathedral beams.

Eli felt fear slip into the spaces between her bones.

The Heart flared up, burning brighter — a lighthouse warning a ship away from a rocky death. But the warning came too late.

The world was called the City of Eyes for a reason.

A ring of white flame encircled the Heart, trapping the four of them inside. Heat licked at their skin, threatening to turn them to ash. Shadows rose up out of the flames, lidless eyes encircled by fire. The first ring of the Coven. The witches whose machinations were killing worlds.

Eli's heart fluttered, and somewhere overhead a fork of lightning danced from branch to branch. This time, if her heart gave out, there would be no one to save her.

She turned her back to the Heart and faced the fire, the Coven, and perhaps her own unmaking.

"I brought them as a gift for the Witch Lord," said Kite, kneeling in supplication to the ring. "The Heart is hungry for flesh."

As Eli watched in disbelief and shock, Kite stepped out of her skin. Her essence joined the white fire.

No, Eli thought wildly. *Not you. Not again.*

A voice rang through her mind, like metal scraping on bone. *You are no one. You are nothing. You were a weapon, and now you are broken. You have no value.*

Eli reached a hand up and felt blood leaking from her ear. She reached for her knives — pearl maybe, or glass? Her hand fell on the empty sheath and panic jolted up her spine.

Her glass blade had been shattered.

Your knives are useless against us, said the voice. *Give yourself to the flame. Only then will you be cleansed. Only then will you be free.*

Trembling uncontrollably, Eli drew the pearl blade across her own palm. Her hand skated wildly, drawing an uneven cut in the flesh. As the blade tore matter from magic, and the light under her skin was exposed to the dark, a different kind of pain seared through her body and woke her from the compulsion.

Beside her, Cam was on all fours, crawling toward the ring of witchfire that would burn him alive. He was crying.

Tav was sweating, hand gripping the obsidian blade. As Eli watched, their hand dropped to their side in defeat. The blade fell to the ground.

Eli could see the nightmares coming to the surface: bruises and broken glass, cigarette butts and bathroom stalls. Only this time, their human fears were changing, growing, metamorphosizing into something else, something terrifying —

The witches were coaxing the memories into life.

Tav coughed raggedly, and sand spilled from their mouth. They were being buried alive.

She had to help them, she had to —

You are nothing. You are no one. You are broken.

The voice pulled her back under, and nothing existed except the voice and her loneliness and the promise of fire.

The stench of burning flesh and rock. Cam had reached the witchfire.

An image cut across her field of vision — the single red scar on Kite's shoulder from the red wind. The scent of oak leaves and rain.

Eli awoke. She threw herself at Cam and wrenched him away from the witchfire, his stones blackened and skin blistering.

"It's so dark," he whispered. He was trembling. He looked at her, but he was seeing someone else. Someone who had hurt him.

She looked around desperately for help. *Kite, Circinae, someone. Anyone.* Lightning flashed above her. Sweat dripped into her eyes.

And finally she understood. No one was coming to save her. She would have to save herself.

She grabbed the obsidian dagger from where it lay near a crooked fiery root and pressed it into Tav's hand. When their hands touched, sparks burst into life.

Tav's pupils slowly focused on Eli. "I'm here," they said.

"Stay with me," said Eli, drawing thorn and stone. She felt the Heart at her back, its wild magic struggling against invisible chains, its lightning as fierce and dangerous as the Coven. She looked at Tav, their human body breathing heavily, their eyes on Eli. They were caught between two powerful magics, and there was only one way out.

Eli faced down the witchfire. She stabbed the thorn blade into the earth, and a rose bush with long sharp spines burst into life and raced furiously toward the flames. The thorns breached the flame, and the fire flickered weakly. Eli's heart soared.

The roses caught fire. The flame ran along the thorns to the hilt of the blade and jumped to Eli's hand.

Pain blocked out everything else.

There was no love or hate or fear. Only pain.

There was no hope or regret or revenge. Only pain.

A single thought broke through, like a lullaby in a minor key. *The Heart is hungry.*

Kite was trying to tell her something. But Kite was part of the flame, the Heir to the Coven, the girl who had danced with Eli under a pink moon.

The Heart.

Eli turned and stared up at the great tree.

We feed broken weapons to the Heart, Circinae had told her.

Circinae had taught her how to read and thrown her into the universe to escape the Coven's fury. Circinae had hurt her, lied to her, used her for her entire life. There were no easy answers. Nothing was certain. But time had finally run out, and she had a choice to make.

As she stepped toward the trunk, a stray spark singed a strand of her hair, and she felt the angry bite of a wounded animal.

It could burn her or drown her or save her.

"What are you doing?!" Tav's voice crawled through the space. It sounded like it came from far away.

She made a choice.

Eli touched the Heart.

Forty-Three

Eli felt heat and a new kind of pain. She looked down to see her bark peeling off in blackened, charcoal curls.

She was being punished.

No, the Heart was being punished, and somehow she was the Heart.

The pain dulled, and Eli felt something new — the absence of something that should be there, like a phantom limb. She was looking, searching for it, but it was out of reach. Something had been lost, forgotten, while the Heart was trapped in the darkness. There were places its roots no longer touched. The pain of this forgetting was tattooed on her soul.

Other images flashed through her mind — she was rain-soaked and dirty, shivering outside a charcoal door that wouldn't open. Her children were bleeding the sap from her great trunk and drinking its power. She was standing alone on the island waiting for someone who wasn't coming. She watched as her children wounded one another and turned away from her light. She was alone. She was alone. She was alone.

She was not alone.

Eli felt the fear and hurt and anger surging through the Heart. And underneath the fury, there was a question. Eli wasn't the only being who was struggling for freedom.

And sometimes we don't have to struggle alone. Sometimes we need each other.

Yes.

The visions faded. She was back in the Coven, surrounded by witchfire. The husk of a great tree stood before her, its leaves blackened by rot and decay. She knew that it was empty, a dead shell.

Her entire body was glowing. She was brighter than the flames, brighter than the gold flecks in Tav's eyes. She was the brightest thing in the world.

"Eli."

She looked up. Tav was staring at her, wide-eyed.

"Take it."

Tav handed Eli the obsidian blade.

Eli walked to the witchfire and cut through the smoke. Cut into the shared essences of the first ring. She had seen a witch die. She knew they could be killed. She was an assassin, an artist of death.

The essences screamed.

The witchfire flickered out, leaving only smouldering embers and ash in a circle around three sweaty bodies and a dead tree.

The witches were fleeing.

The essences of the witches that made up the first ring re-formed outside the dead circle, no longer joined. Balls of light, of energy, wavering and trembling at the sight of the glowing girl. They were afraid.

But they would fight back, and Eli couldn't fight them all. The Heart had been locked down here for too long, and the vicious magic of the chains that had bound her yearned to wrap themselves around her ankles and keep her here forever. She had been weakened by the shearing of her roots, by the burning of the forest, by the breaking of a glass blade. She was vulnerable.

And the Heart had a human body now, and bodies were fragile. Already hairline cracks were reopening along an arm that had recently been broken.

Eli turned to her companions. Now that the ring had been broken, Cam was breathing more steadily and struggling to stand up. Tav wiped the sweat from their face, leaving a streak of ash behind. They spat out a mouthful of sand and grimaced. They were both readying themselves for another fight, and it made her heart ache.

"Tav?" Her voice was heavy with fatigue, but the question was tinged with hope. She offered them the obsidian knife. When Tav took it, Eli sent a surge of honeygold power into their body — sharing the power of the Heart, the power of the world. Then Eli gripped their wrist tightly. "You can do this," she said. Tav reached out with their free hand to take Cam's.

Eli's hand fell to the fragment of china that still hung around her neck. *Please, please let this work. Take us somewhere safe.*

Tav reached for the threads of magic that wove the world.

A door opened.

Forty-Four

They fell for eternity.

Eli saw the junkyard of lost and discarded things. Something in her reached out to it, but it was too late —

They fell through stone, through the underbelly of the Labyrinth, through tree roots and fossils.

For a moment, Tav, Cam, and Eli hung over Earth. The planet was a beautiful and broken piece of glassware, cracked and glittering with millions of gold lights. It looked very fragile. Then it was gone, and they were falling again.

Doors kept opening and closing, images rushing by as they fell through the City of Eyes again and again and again.

Tav was panicking. They needed a safe haven.

Eli squeezed Tav's hand, sending a glittering thread of power from her hand to theirs. Tav grabbed for the knife at their belt and tried to shove it into a doorway, to drag them out of the tunnel and into a space — something, anything. It slipped through brick and stone and wood and bone, caught on patches of spirit and shadow and gaps in the world, but skittered off as they kept falling down, down, down.

"Breathe," whispered Eli. "You can do this."

Eli watched as Tav took a deep breath and closed their eyes. The magic crackled and swirled around them. She could see the tension in their shoulders and neck from a lifetime of fear and fury. Eli wanted to smooth that tension away, to kiss the base of their neck, even as she remembered the way the witch had been torn open at their touch.

She pressed the chip of bone china, the pendant gifted to her by a child of the Labyrinth, into their hand.

"Take us here," said Eli.

Colours and light flashed around Tav, moving through their body, the magic threads mapping a spectrum of wild and messy emotions. In one quick movement, Tav threw the pendant into the void as both sacrifice and anchor.

A moment later, they collapsed on a stone floor.

"Took you long enough," said Clytemnestra. "Did you really steal the Heart?" She seemed smaller than last time, almost toddler sized. Her exaggerated Cupid's bow mouth was twisted into a sneer.

"Hi, baby demon," said Tav, struggling for breath. They shoved their hands into their hair, trying to push the wilted spikes back into place.

The glow of the Heart had dulled, but Eli could still feel it in her blood. Everything was brighter, sharper, stranger. Even without her magical eyes, she could see magic everywhere. It was overwhelming.

Clytemnestra was eyeing her like she was dessert. "Tasty," she said and licked her lips. Eli was too exhausted to respond.

"We need to get back to Earth," said Tav. "Can you help us?"

"I can," said Clytemnestra, rocking back and forth. "But that doesn't mean I will." She giggled.

Tav raised the black dagger.

"Threats already? Ooh, you *are* going to be fun!" Clytemnestra stretched onto her tiptoes and turned a pirouette. "But you can't go yet. You'll miss it."

"Miss what?"

They were interrupted by the sound of a thousand trees screaming — not in pain but in anger. Under the roots were deep stones, the teeth of the world, and for a moment they all understood that the Labyrinth was the mouth of the world, and then the sound ended, and the understanding passed.

Clytemnestra bent over to touch her toes and then stared up at Tav as she hung there, head between her legs. "The war party, of course." She skipped off, vanishing into thin air.

A doorway opened in the walls, and Cam, Eli, and Tav stumbled through it. The walls continued to change as they moved through space. Cam, who seemed to instinctively know where to go, led the way. He was guided by the stone walls that recognized him as part of them.

Eli trailed behind the others, keeping watch. She and the Children's Lair were like two beasts greeting one another with grudging respect. She didn't know what to expect from a war party — not sugar cookies this time.

Finally, they came to a large, open chamber. It was filled with little witches. Poisonous berries and spiky flowers that looked like weapons grew out of cracks in the floor. Blankets and broken toys had been pushed to the sides of the room. In one corner, a giant marionette danced with the grace of a prima ballerina. Eli looked up. Great ghostly branches stretched across a bleak sky — dark grey with one violent streak of orange. Clytemnestra floated like a star in the centre of the room. When she spoke, the sound echoed through the chamber.

"I am the voice of the children, the oldest and youngest of us, the Warlord who will lead us to victory."

Shifting beside Cam, Eli frowned. *Clytemnestra? The Warlord?* What was going on?

"We have been children for generations. We have watched witches grow and forget about us, forget the pact we made with the dirt and the mud, forget how to speak to magic and instead only consume it. We have watched and revelled in their violence, but their violence is no longer chaotic and creative and life-giving. The Coven has become meticulous and measured. That is a death sentence to us, our way of life, and our world.

"The Labyrinth has been under attack for a long time, and its roots have weakened. We are no longer safe hiding here. It is time to come out of hiding and begin our open attack on the Coven. It is time for the children to claim our heritage!"

The children cheered, banging pots and pans together, scraping knives against stone. Someone was lighting foul-smelling fires that reached up toward the sky.

"We are mischief makers, and we make mischief for the Coven. We will be the troublemakers who play with the trees and dance on our parents' bones!

"Today a victory was won — we have captured the Heart of the World."

Now the children were quiet, curious, looking around and whispering. One bit into a piece of fruit and let the black juice dribble down his chin.

"The Heart has powers that even the Coven has never fully understood. And now that it is free, it will help us break the Coven!"

"Break! Break! Break!" chanted the children. The only thing more fun than building a castle was knocking it down.

"The assassin and her companions have also brought us an old weapon, from before the moon war, rescued from the wastelands." Clytemnestra held up a strange instrument: a long metal rod studded with curved and spiky arms and the occasional toothy gear. The children oohed and aahed.

"My staff!" gasped Cam.

"She tricked us," whispered Tav, admiration creeping into their voice.

"Tonight we dance." Clytemnestra gave a wolfish smile. "And tomorrow we fight!"

More squeals and screams of delight. A broken record player spontaneously blasted a rock anthem. Someone picked up a fiddle. Suddenly everyone was dancing, swirling in complicated patterns, laughing and falling over each other. Eli was caught up in the whirlwind of bodies that grabbed at her hair and arms and legs. But she wasn't a child anymore, and the dance only made her dizzy. She felt the hairline fracture in her arm split and gritted her teeth in pain. The Children's revels were dangerous, and Kite was no longer around to heal her.

Cam pulled her out of the sea of children. "Let's go."

She nodded and let him lead her and Tav away from the revel. Before stepping through the wall, she turned back, looking for laburnum and lace, for a valentine mouth and vampire smile.

But Clytemnestra was nowhere to be seen.

Forty-Five

"We need to heal the wounds between worlds," said Tav. "I think with my magic and Eli's new Heart we can. We have to try." The passion had returned to their voice, their words scarlet and indigo and copper.

"The Coven will be coming for us," said Cam, polishing a chip of sandstone on his forearm.

"Let them come." Eli's hand twitched toward her knives, her thumb brushing gently over the empty sheath. They would pay for that.

"What about Kite? She's with the Coven now." Cam glanced sideways at Eli.

"I don't know. I don't know if she's working with them or not." Eli frowned, remembering her words at the end. *The Heart is hungry.* Had she known what would happen if Eli touched the Heart?

"So we forget about her for now," said Tav. "It doesn't matter."

It mattered to Eli, but she knew they didn't have time to unravel the mystery of her closest and least trusted friend.

"We stay here tonight," said Eli, "and tomorrow we go back to the City of Ghosts. We fix this."

They agreed.

Long after Cam had fallen asleep, Eli was still awake, picking at scabs of worry.

"What are you thinking?" The gold in Tav's eyes seemed to brighten when they were looking at Eli. Or maybe it was the Heart they were looking at.

"Are you going to hand me over to the Hedge-Witch?" said Eli.

"She wants to use it for good."

"She wants to use *me*. I'm not an *it*. And not everyone thinks it's good, what you want to do. You've seen how dangerous magic can be. Is that really what you want for your city?"

Tav's eyes slid down Eli's body for a moment, at the made-thing that was also the Heart. Eli imagined them thirsting for the magic and power in her cartilage and shifted away.

"I don't know. If it was used by the right person —"

"You can't know who will use it."

Silence.

"She would use me. *You* would use me," Eli pushed.

"Maybe." Tav's eyes fell to their lap. "Yes. Eli — we could use your magic to help people."

"The Heart belongs in this world."

"Maybe it doesn't. You don't know that for sure."

Eli let the silence grow, building walls between them. She wanted to reach out and touch them, but she held back. She needed to know. "So what are you going to do when we get back?"

Tav ran their thumb along the flat of the obsidian blade. They sighed. Raised their head. "I'm going to do what I said. Help save Earth. After that ... well, we'll see."

"Yes," Eli agreed sadly, "we'll see."

She didn't sleep. She was still afraid of what she might dream. She couldn't wait to get back to the City of Ghosts. She was so tired.

Once Tav was asleep, Eli stood. The wall melted before her, welcoming her deeper into the Children's Lair. Eli walked through it.

Clytemnestra was waiting.

"I'd say thank you," Eli said, "but you used me. You knew what we were doing. You wanted us to steal the Heart. You wanted us to work for you all along."

"You want to leave, leave. Let the world die." Clytemnestra shrugged.

"You know I can't do that."

"Do I?" Clytemnestra chewed on her thumbnail. "The old Eli would have."

Eli said nothing to that. "I don't owe you anything anymore. You saved my life, and I stole the Heart. Damaged your enemies."

"And you'll keep helping us."

"We'll keep fighting the Coven."

Clytemnestra inclined her head. "Close enough." She grinned. Her lips stretched gruesomely, showing off every tooth. They had been filed to razor-sharp edges. It really was true then — the children were going to war. "You no longer owe me for saving your life. It's a fair trade."

Eli shifted from one foot to the other. "We're not staying. We have to heal the rifts."

"Oh, I know." Clytemnestra tossed her hair. "You won't be able to come back without a token. Want another present?" Clytemnestra pulled a long golden hair from her head and offered it to Eli with a sly smile.

Eli shook her head. "No more tricks. No more debts."

Clytemnestra floated forward and patted Eli on the head. "There are always more tricks. But don't worry, we'll see you again. When we storm the Coven, there will be no need for the children to hide in the Labyrinth."

Eli nodded, wondering what the City of Eyes would look like when Clytemnestra had razed the Coven to the ground.

Clytemnestra pinched the loose skin around Eli's elbow. A sensation like warm honey spread up Eli's arm as it healed.

"I help you and you help me." The baby witch giggled. "That's what friends do!"

"I already paid for the healing. You owed it to me." Eli's smile was more like a snarl.

"What?" Clytemnestra frowned.

Eli reached into the pocket of Clytemnestra's pinafore and pulled out a silver earring. "Last time we met, I gave you this gift. Don't you remember?"

Still smiling, she backed away from the witch, never letting Clytemnestra out of her line of sight. Even tiny Warlords were dangerous.

Eli spent the next few hours watching over her companions. Now that the Coven had released their nightmares, she was worried their dreams would no longer be safe. But neither of them dreamed at all. Eli wondered what that meant. Had the witches damaged their ability to dream?

Finally, the night ended, and a new day began somewhere in the City of Ghosts.

Here the sky was greypink, pale and sticky. Eli wondered when she would see these skies again. She wasn't in a hurry to come back.

Clytemnestra cast glamours on Eli and Cam to hide their strangeness in the human world. "Heal the wounds," the Warlord said, "and your debt to me will be paid."

"If we manage that, you will owe us a thousand glamours," said Eli.

"*When*, not *if*," said Tav.

The Warlord burst into tears and fumbled in her pinafore until she found a stained handkerchief. "I hate goodbyes!" she sobbed.

They had decided to reopen Clytemnestra's stitch, the one the impish witch used to sneak between worlds without the Coven's knowledge. Eli was itching to see

Tav make their own pathway between worlds instead of manipulating witch magic, but she didn't want to push them. Not yet. In the battles to come, Tav's newfound abilities would be pressed to their limits.

As Eli waited to cross, she felt a twinge of cold along the healed fracture of her arm. It was weakened and would rebreak more easily now. Eli would have to be careful.

"God, I can't wait for coffee," groaned Cam. "I've been in caffeine withdrawal since we left."

Eli smiled at him. At least in the struggles ahead, there would be coffee.

"You kids ready to be impressed?" Tav had talked Clytemnestra into fixing their hair — the purple strands stuck up in spikes again.

"Always," said Eli.

"Sure, Sonic."

Tav reached into the air and unraveled the seam. Storm clouds whipped around their elbow and the temperature dropped.

"Deadly assassins first," they said to Eli, bowing.

She stepped through the door.

Forty-Six

Eli popped an extra-strength Advil and downed it with a mouthful of espresso. The weight of a granite spine was hell on a human body, even one that was infused with the Heart of another world. But she would never be turned back into the parts the witch had used to make her — a girl stitched together out of pearl and glass, obsidian and blood laced with control.

Eli was in control now. She looked down at her bare arm, admiring the pathways of veins, waterways that flowed across stone and wood and earth and flesh. For a moment, her veins lit up with a golden glow, a constellation dancing across her skin, a reminder of the magic that was now a part of her body.

Eli wasn't just a teenage girl with fingerprints on her glasses and freckles on her shoulders. Eli was a refugee from another world, a warrior, friend, and lover. A girl who loved reading romance novels and hated dust mites, who moved with grace and strength, and who was still healing from the wounds of her childhood.

She was a person.

"Can you taste the pineapple?" asked Cam. The apartment smelled like coffee grounds and old books, and Eli already loved it more than the cottage she had grown up in.

"No." She let her arm drop to her side. The blades chimed softly at her hips: frost, bone, thorn, stone, and pearl. The blades were a part of her.

Two were missing.

One broken, forever lost to her.

The other entrusted to someone Eli couldn't stop thinking about.

"We need to work on your palate." Cam pushed another espresso mug toward her. "Try again. And sip it this time — it's not a shot."

"It's called a shot," she pointed out.

"Who's being shot?" A sleepy tenor wound its way through the apartment.

Eli tried not to stare. Tav was wearing a pair of grey sweatpants and an oversized white tee. Their short hair flopped over to one side of their face, and silver earrings ran the length of both ears. A slender dagger of black glass was strapped to one forearm, obscuring a tattoo that Eli wanted to ask about.

Eli swallowed. "Um. Hey."

"That for me?" Tav took the espresso shot and tipped it back. The obsidian blade chimed in answer to its sisters.

"That's *not* how you're supposed to drink it." Cam sighed.

Tav shrugged, setting the mug back on the counter, fingers inches from Eli's elbow. Eli felt her heart race, and then —

Something *happened*.

Tav's eyes widened. "Eli?"

"What?" Eli tilted her head to one side and smiled. Her elbow slid over the countertop and brushed Tav's fingertips. She tucked her other arm behind her back.

Tav frowned. "It's just … it's like you were here, and then you weren't. Just for, like, a nanosecond. Like, you *flickered*. I could almost see *through* you —"

Eli laughed nervously. "You need to get more sleep."

"Always. Did you sleep?"

"Yeah."

"You both slept forever," complained Cam. "And I'm hungry. It's your turn to make breakfast."

Tav watched Eli for a few moments and then nodded slowly. They turned to Cam. "Move over — I'd hate for you to get gravel in the batter. Pancakes? Waffles?"

"Pancakes."

Eli turned her back to her friends and opened her hand. Her palm was still transparent.

Pure light.

This new body would take some getting used to.

As Cam and Tav bickered playfully over the flour and vanilla, Eli wandered over to the window. She looked out at the human city haunted by the ghosts of a dead moon. She thought about the way trauma bleeds over edges, across bodies and stars and planets. She thought about the dying Earth and her dead mother and the two hearts that burned in her alien body. She thought about how much would have to change for the violence to end and wondered if three small bodies could really mend a broken world.

Tomorrow, she told herself, turning away from the city and toward Cam and Tav. People who cared for her, needed her, believed in her. They weren't running from the fight, and neither was she. *We start tomorrow.*

Wounds could heal. That much she knew.

What the Humans Left Behind

Somewhere outside the city was a picturesque cottage with a thatched roof, round windows, and a jaunty hand-painted sign that read The Sun.

Inside, potted plants waved their magic tentacles while the Hedge-Witch paced back and forth. "They've been gone too long," she said. "Something's gone wrong."

"We should send someone after them."

The Hedge-Witch ignored the suggestion. Only Tav could carry humans across worlds. She had felt their magic the first time they met, the silver glow of witching essence pulsing under their eyelids.

She stopped to soothe an agitated succulent, lightly running her fingers along its skin. "It's okay, baby," she whispered. "I'll protect you."

The humans watched her, waiting.

She could see the colours of feeling burning under the skin of each human. Fear. Worry. Anger. In their eyes, she had failed. Whispers swirled around the room — although whether they were words spoken with crooked human tongues or simply thoughts fluttering free from the confines of a leaking mind, she did not know.

What if they're dead?

We need that magic.

She promised us.

Without the Heart, how can we change anything?

Since when had she become a beacon of hope for the lonely? When had she become responsible for the lives and wishes of such fragile creatures? They craved her guidance, clung to it. They wanted her magic.

Her mouth salivated with the sweet and bitter taste of power, like almond and orange peel.

The Hedge-Witch sighed and reached for her mug of chamomile tea. She added a spoonful of honey, the crystallized coppery sweetness still buzzing with the memory of wings. A sprig of lavender. A rusted iron nail. She took a sip.

Calm radiated through her body.

Where was Tav's ghost? The creature had followed them willingly, had protected them. Would he work for her, follow her directions, now that Tav was gone?

Not *he*, *it*. It was a ghost. She had spent too much time with Tav and was starting to think of it as a person. Where was it now? Waiting at a closed-down bus station, wading in the river, watching The Sun with dead eyes? What would it do when Tav didn't return?

A sense of foreboding fell across her forehead like a shadow.

She looked up and faced her followers, their eyes desperate for a story. "The Coven will be coming for us. We need to prepare." Had they been killed? Would it bother her to learn that Tav had died, after all the time she had spent with them? But then humans died so easily, like crickets.

"The Coven?"

"*Here?*"

"Cam would never tell them about us!"

"Babe, it'll be okay." A woman with dark braids brushed a human hand against a non-human arm. The air between them rippled like water.

"The trace spell I planted on them is broken." The Hedge-Witch took her lover's hand and kissed it. Her lips left behind the shape of the kiss in orange rust. "Something terrible has happened. I can smell it in the air. I can taste it in the dirt. My dreams are broken. The Heart has changed, and the City of Eyes is changing, too. Magic feels different — the texture is coarser and harder to grasp. You wouldn't understand." She sighed again. Sometimes she missed the company of other witches. "Something has changed, but it isn't what we had planned."

In the moments that followed, the cacophony of human bodies pounded in the Hedge-Witch's ears — their twitching eyelashes, shifting joints, grinding teeth. She could hear their skin shedding and growing, their bones rotating in imperfect sockets.

She took another sip of tea. That helped.

"What do we do?" someone asked nervously.

"We should never have trusted that witch-made creature."

"Don't worry," said the Hedge-Witch soothingly. She reached out and stroked a flowering cactus. "We can still get the Heart. This isn't over. We just have to find the girl."

She swallowed the rest of the tea in one gulp, catching the nail between her teeth. She bit down on the iron, letting her tongue graze the tip. Blood summoned blood.

The door swung open.

A girl walked in, steely eyes panning the room. Two swords were strapped across her back. One cobbled together from broken bottles and Phillips-head screws. A weapon meant to wound rather than kill. A cruel edge. The other crafted from thousands of iridescent insect wings. The sound of a swarm of wasps followed the blade. It was restless.

The Hedge-Witch took the nail from her mouth and set it delicately in her empty cup.

"You didn't think Eli was the only one, did you?"

She turned to her made-girl, the project she had finally completed after all this time. She offered her daughter three strands of hair, sticky with saliva.

"Find her."

Acknowledgements

I owe so much to the amazing Dundurn team, who brought this adventure from YA NOVEL DRAFT 3.docx to printed book. Thank you to Rachel Spence, who read the first chaotic draft and saw something in it. Thank you to Jenny McWha, Chrissy Calhoun, and Shari Rutherford for polishing the story and making sure we knew the recipe for Eli's body. Thank you to Elham Ali and the marketing team for sharing my story with readers. Thank you to Laura Boyle and the design team, especially Sophie Paas-Lang, for the beautiful cover design. I will never stop fanboying over it.

A thousand thank yous to my incredible editor, Whitney French, who guided me through every writing crisis with tea and *Avatar: The Last Airbender* references. This book would not exist without your thoughtful insights and suggestions.

Thank you to my sister, Haven, who was my first audience and fan. We shared a bedroom growing up, and I used to tell her stories about fairies, princesses, and magic teenagers. She would always remember the characters' names and ask me what happened next. Haven is also the first person in my family I came out to as nonbinary, and she has been so incredibly supportive. I love you so much.

Thank you to my mom for always encouraging me to read and write — and for making mimosas when I found out that my book had been accepted.

Thank you to my early readers and magical bookish friends who told me after ten pages that they would read more: Zoe Lyons, Ingrid Doell, Matthew Scott Wilson, and Jack Morton.

Thank you to my cat Dragon for being patient with me when I didn't have time to play, and for mostly sleeping on my lap instead of my keyboard.

Thank you to Rida Abu Rass for the playlist "Weird mixtape for cute authors editing their books" <3.

Thank you to the queer book club in Hamilton where I first felt accepted using they/them pronouns, to the baristas in all the indie cafés where I wrote and edited, and to all the angry feminists doing their thing.

Finally, I want to write a bit about what it means to be a Canadian author living and writing in Canada. I grew up in Kingston, Ontario, on the traditional lands of the Haudenosaunee and Anishinaabe nations, sixty-five kilometres from Tyendinaga Mohawk Territory.

As a Canadian author, it's important to recognize the Indigenous Peoples living on the land they have always cared for and to respect the rights and sovereignty of these nations. I did not write about Indigenous struggles in my book, but I encourage all readers — especially those in Canada — to think and learn more about our relationship to each other and to the land and to support Indigenous girls, women, and two-spirit people.

ELI AND TAV
ARE BACK
IN

The

Boi of

Feather

and Steel

COMING
SUMMER 2021

READ ON FOR
AN EXCERPT!

Tav

Tav was dreaming.

The river was frozen over with thick black ice. When they knelt down, they could see blue-and-white flames trapped under the surface. They placed a palm over the ice, feeling the cold burn like fire. The flames flickered wildly, trying to reach their hand.

A hairline crack snaked its way between their feet. Tav stepped back, uneasy. As they watched in horror, the river tore itself in two, ice and water and earth splitting apart. Tav stumbled and fell, narrowly avoiding the spears of ice stabbing the air like a fractured bone puncturing skin.

A great chasm stretched across the frozen river. Tav found themselves on one side of the fierce water, which gushed through a cracked mirror of black ice.

A boy climbed out of the depths of a world splintered by frost and starlight.

Cam. Eyes like stone, hard and cold. Blue veins glistening under exposed skin.

Cradled in his arms lay the crumpled body of a girl, a sprig of hawthorn growing from her chest.

She was dying.

"I brought your heart," he said, stepping onto Tav's side of the river. The curve of his smile was a fishhook. He stopped an arms' length from where Tav crouched, their fingernails etching lines into the crystalline landscape. He waited.

Tav rose slowly, unsteady on their feet. Sweat dripped down their neck. They could smell rot.

Pain surged through their shoulder blades. They cried out as great feathered wings burst from their back. The wings were black as ink, with an oily lustre of gold and purple and green. As the pain began to subside like a waning crescent moon, Tav found Cam's eyes and forced the breath from their lungs into the shape of a single command.

"Give her to me."

"You've left me no choice," he said. His fingers curled around hawthorn, twisting brutally. The girl whimpered.

"Let her go!" Tav beat their wings, and white flames burned through the ice at their feet. The ice floe was unstable, and one wrong move could lead to hypothermia and drowning. The stars glittered overhead, their lights reflected in the dark mirror. The universe was burning.

The branch snapped, and the girl screamed, a body made of bone and glass crying out in agony.

Tav lunged, nails like talons curving around Cam's throat.

When it was over, Tav was on all fours, frost licking their knees. Blood everywhere. Body parts were scattered across the ice. Tav wetted their lips and looked down, catching a glimpse of their reflection —

the face of a witch

Tav woke suddenly and found themselves back in their apartment, the sheets soaked through with sweat. In the dim room lit only by distant streetlights, the shadows looked like blood. Tav fumbled for the bedside lamp. When the yellow pool of light showed no evidence of a crime scene, the anxiety curling its claws around their wrists and ankles released its hold. It was just a dream; it was already fading. Tav listened to the sound of their pounding heart, waiting for the rhythm to slow. Proof that they were human.

Tav closed their eyes against the pain of sudden brightness, but it was too late. Already a headache was spreading through their temples and pushing into the corded muscles of their neck.

They switched off the light and lay back down, opening their eyes to the dark. In the distance, sirens sang out, the clear, sharp pitch breaking through the dull roar of engines that never ceased. Threaded through the darkness was the magic of the Heart, which wound its way through walls and doors and flesh and bone. Tav fought the urge to reach out and grab it, to make themselves strong, to heal their pain, to take that power all for themselves and use it.

Use *her*.

Eli was sleeping on the couch, separated by only a wall. The thought sent another shiver of excitement through Tav's body, but of a different kind. They kicked off the lounge pants they'd fallen asleep in and lay back in their boxers. Eli's hair would be messy, her body tangled in the blanket. Tav remembered her body; they had followed the path of her collarbone with their mouth, traced the curve of her waist with their hand ...

Tav rolled their face into the pillow to stifle a moan. They lost themselves to fantasy before sleep finally returned for them.

In the morning they had forgotten about the dream.